Modern Critical Interpretations

John Gay's
The Beggar's Opera

Modern Critical Interpretations

These and other titles in preparation

Modern Critical Interpretations

John Gay's
The Beggar's Opera

Edited and with an introduction by

Harold Bloom
Sterling Professor of the Humanities
Yale University

Chelsea House Publishers ◊ *1988*
NEW YORK ◊ NEW HAVEN ◊ PHILADELPHIA

© 1988 by Chelsea House Publishers, a division
of Chelsea House Educational Communications, Inc.

Introduction © 1988 by Harold Bloom

Printed and bound in the United States of America

10 9 8 7 6 5 4 3 2 1

∞ The paper used in this publication meets the minimum
requirements of the American National Standard for
Permanence of Paper for Printed Library Materials,
Z39.48-1984

Library of Congress Cataloging-in-Publication Data
John Gay's The beggar's opera / edited and with an
introduction by Harold Bloom.
    p. cm.—(Modern critical interpretations)
  Bibliography: p.
  Includes index.
  ISBN 0-87754-419-0 (alk. paper) : $19.95
  1. Gay, John, 1685–1732. Beggar's opera. I. Bloom,
Harold. II. Series.
PR3473.B6J64 1988   87-27631
822'.5—dc19   CIP

Contents

Editor's Note

This book brings together a representative selection of the best modern critical interpretations of John Gay's *The Beggar's Opera*. The critical essays are reprinted here in the chronological order of their original publication. I am grateful to Edward Jefferson and Susan Laity for their aid in editing this volume.

My introduction speculates upon the relationship of *The Beggar's Opera* to what Freud called the "reality principle." The late Sir William Empson properly begins the chronological sequence of criticism with his fecund observations upon *The Beggar's Opera* as one of the major versions of pastoral. In Martin Price's equally acute commentary, the portrait of Polly forms an interesting contrast to Empson's.

Patricia Meyer Spacks, celebrating Gay's major work as an assured triumph, emphasizes the opera's double view of the world as being simultaneously ridiculous and horrifying. Ronald Paulson briefly examines how the language of commerce makes of the play a comedy of manners.

For William A. McIntosh, the opera's duality is not one of aims, satirizing Walpole the Whig as well as Handel and Italian opera, since McIntosh argues that these supposed aims have been exaggerated and count for much less than Gay's didactic purposes in his social satire. Peter Lewis also explores Gay's "satire" of the Italian opera, showing how Gay deliberately orders the piece as an opera and, by this organization, creates an anti- or parody opera. Michael Denning centers on the ideology of the gang and sees the struggle in *Beggar's Opera* as being "between two types of law, the one represented by the reprieve, the other by poetical justice." This volume concludes with John Fuller's· overview of the play, which points out that Gay's use of mixed genres is wholly appropriate for an opera written by a beggar.

Introduction

William Empson, with amiable irony, said of *The Beggar's Opera* that its glory was "to give itself so wholeheartedly to vulgarization." The acute word there is "wholeheartedly," and that is the truer glory of John Gay's durable opera, ancestor of Gilbert and Sullivan and of Brecht's *Threepenny Opera*. It is so wholehearted a work (like the rest of Gay) that it runs off and away from Gay's utmost intentions and very nearly becomes an artistic heterocosm, a little world of its own, endlessly cheerful, yet always shadowed by betrayal, the pox, and the gallows. Martin Price finds in the "ironic flexibility and detachment" of Gay a precise anticipation of Brecht's celebrated "alienation effect," and Gay indeed is much more complex in his design and stance than the Marxist Brecht chose to be.

The Beggar's Opera is a benign first cousin of *The Dunciad* and *A Tale of a Tub,* and, though a "Newgate pastoral," remains a kind of pastoral, as Empson classically demonstrated: "It is [the] clash and identification of the refined, the universal, and the low that is the whole point of the pastoral." Mock-pastoral, in Empson's vision, fostered a code of independence. Rereading *The Beggar's Opera,* after listening to a good recorded performance of it, oppresses me rather (it is the only oppression involved) with a sense of how dependent everyone in Gay's world truly is, where you escape no consequence of your actions, whether illegal or immoral, except in the grand and unlikely reprieve that the Beggar-poet is obliged to grant. Lockit, Peachum, Macheath, Filch, the gang, are not less dependent upon the underworld system and economy than are Mrs. Peachum, Polly, Lucy, Diana Trapes, and those eight vivid whores of whom Jenny Diver is the most interesting. Everyone is splen-

1

didly capable of hanging everyone else, no man is far from the gallows and no woman from transportation. Yet the marvelous good humor, zest for life, general high spirits, and fantastic bravura are unmatched in literature between Villon and Babel's *Tales of Odessa*. Like Villon and Babel, Gay has a clear sense of the abyss and knows well that his dance of life is always just a step away from a dance of death.

Gay's sense of the absurd owes something to his good friends Swift and Pope, but his sense of potential punishment or anxious expectations is essentially his own. Technically Peachum is the opera's villain, and Macheath its hero, but they agree upon everything that matters, have the same values and the same fatalism. Peachum, being older and wiser, plays it safer; Macheath is the more overt gambler and knows himself to be compulsive about women. What they share most crucially is a knowledge manifested, to a lesser degree, by everyone else in the opera. To keep going in a dangerous existence (and this opera intends to teach us that all existence is dangerous), you require a rhetoric of self-justification and indeed self-exaltation. You need never misrepresent your motives, whether to yourself or to others, but you must elevate your language when you apply it to your own status or function in the economy, psychic or social. That rhetorical elevation need not be assigned to others, though that is the true division between Peachum and Macheath. Peachum and Mrs. Peachum rarely address Polly without calling her a slut or hussy, and Lockit does as well with Lucy. Macheath, in everything he says to his gang or his women, is as nobly rhetorical as the hero of romance he knows himself not to be.

Polly and Lucy, as Martin Price remarks, are necessarily their father's daughters and are quite formidable women, as Macheath discovers. If the gallant captain truly loves anyone in the opera, she appears to be Jenny Diver, who betrays him as a lowlife Cleopatra should, with style and without regret. Gay, never forgetting that his genre was operatic satire, declined to develop any of his women (or men, for that matter) more complexly than his plot required. Yet there is a curious wistfulness in Macheath. Gay clearly felt the attractions with which he had endowed the feckless mock-aristocratic highwayman, but he had the aesthetic restraint to circumscribe his own sympathy and so keep our sympathy for Macheath from becoming at all serious.

Still, Macheath is no Mack the Knife, just as Peachum is finally too engaging, in his gusto and mercenary intensity, to be less than a good-natured satire upon Walpole, who had the wit to attend, just once, and to call for an encore at the right moment. Gay swerved from Macheath at the right moment, since to execute the hero would have ruined the opera, despite the Beggar-poet's call for "strict poetical justice." Peachum and Lockit are indeed, as Macheath says, infamous scoundrels, but we don't want them hanged anymore than we want to see Macheath hanged. In his farewell to representatives of the gang, Macheath is on the edge of turning comic opera into tragicomedy, when he tells his men, "look well to yourselves, for in all probability you may live some months longer." We prefer Peachum's opening aria:

> Through all the employments of life,
>   Each neighbour abuses his brother;
> Whore and rogue they call husband and wife:
>   All professions be-rogue one another.
> The priest calls the lawyer a cheat,
>   The lawyer be-knaves the divine;
> And the statesman, because he's so great,
>   Thinks his trade as honest as mine.

That is Gay's true note: exuberantly outrageous and faithful to the reality principle that governs the opera, without, however, abandoning itself to that principle. The highest praise I can render Gay is that he returns us to Shakespeare's Falstaff and Falstaff's cosmos. Peachum is no Falstaff and Macheath no Hotspur, but Falstaff's vision of reality (though not his awesome wit) is revived in *The Beggar's Opera*.

The Beggar's Opera: Mock-pastoral as the Cult of Independence

William Empson

The stock device of the play is a double irony like a Seidlitz powder, piling a dramatic irony onto what was already an irony. This forces one to read back a more complex irony onto the first one, and the composure of language of the characters makes us feel that the speaker took the whole sense for granted. So he is a pastoral character; he moves among fundamental truths. The trick of style that makes this plausible is Comic Primness, the double irony in the acceptance of a convention. This is never meant by the speaker as a single critical irony ("I pretend to agree with this only to make you use your judgment and see that it is wrong")—if an irony does that it does not seem prim—though the author may mean a critical irony when he assigns the character a primness. No sentence of the play is quite free from this trick; one might only doubt over "bring those villains to the gallows before you, and I am satisfied," but though there is plain indignation in both Gay and Macheath, for Macheath to feel it is in a degree "rogue-becoming-judge," funny because self-righteous. One might divide Comic Primness with the usual divisions of comedy, according to the degree to which the inherent criticism is intended.

It may assume that the conventions are right and that to be good is to keep them; by applying them unexpectedly a sense of relief is put into their tightness, though one is still good; they are made to seem deliberately assumed, so that the normal man is unchanged beneath them, and this gives a sense of power and freedom

From *Some Versions of Pastoral.* © 1960 by New Directions.

just as custard-pie farce does. You may say that this simple type assumes the others—"What is an important truth for us would not be true on a higher level; it is good to see the superficiality of the rules we must none the less keep." But this may be inherent and yet well out of sight. This type goes with "free" comedy.

It may imply simply that the conventions are wrong, as a critical irony would, but if it is to remain Comic Primness it must then also imply that the speaker does not feel strong enough, or much desire, perhaps for selfish reasons, to stand up against them; he shelters behind them and feels cosy. One would use this in "critical" comedy, but it would be hard to make a complete critical comedy without ever leaving comic primness.

In full Comic Primness (an element of "full" comedy) the enjoyer gets the joke at both levels—both that which accepts and that which revolts against the convention that the speaker adopts primly. It is a play of judgment which implies not so much doubt as a full understanding of issues between which the enjoyer, with the humility of impertinence, does not propose to decide. For this pleasure of effective momentary simplification the arguments of the two sides must be pulling their weight on the ironist, and though he might be sincerely indignant if told so it is fair to call him conscious of them. A character who accepts this way of thinking tends to be forced into isolation by sheer strength of mind, and so into a philosophy of Independence.

This may be used for Ironical Humility, whose simplest gambit is to say, "I am not clever, educated, well born," or what not (as if you had a low standard to judge by), and then to imply that your standards are so high in the matter that the person you are humbling yourself before is quite out of sight. This has an amusing likeness to pastoral; the important man classes himself among low men, and the effect is to raise his standards, not to lower them. At the stage of "device prior to irony" this is an essential weapon of pastoral. I shall try to show that Polly uses it in this way. Also there is a feeling of ironical humility diffused generally through the play, as if the characters knew they were really much better than heroes and prime ministers, not merely like them, though they do not choose to say so clearly; the reason for this, I think, is that the pretence that Macheath and Walpole are both heroes is a sort of ironical humility in the author ("I am easily impressed"), not so much a critical one as one implying a reserve of force—"by this means I can understand them completely." Such an ironical humility is in effect like the attitude of the scientist; the observer must not alter what he observes but shrink to a mere eye. A man like Boswell writes of himself like this because he wants to keep himself out of the scene of which in fact he was the stage manager. The richness of the ironical humility of Chaucer is that he combines the truth-seeking feeling in the trick with its poetical one of pastoral (the notion that a rightly conducted love affair is a means of understanding the world seems to hold the two together). The ironical humility of Samuel Butler is a more curious matter. It aims at outflanking the official moralists, making their pomposity absurd by giving similar but different moral advice under cover of giving merely practical advice. "Every system leads to absurdity in extreme cases, so we must be careful to keep our system to plain obvious cases"; "we must avoid the ideal and extreme because we have been taught false ideals." He cannot help thinking about higher matters than he pretends to, but this acts as a criticism of language; "the words of all moralists shift as mine do, only they have not the sense to see it. I may not be doing much but I am keeping my head." That is the force of the perpetual analogy from business to spiritual matters, and the double irony of his sustained praise of the "mean." (He does not try to stop altering the field in the course of observing it by making himself small but uses the alterations for further knowledge.) "Pray let nobody idealise *me*"; the whole charm of his trick, and it is a genuine one, is that he refuses to recognise the grandeur of the senses which he cannot keep out of his words. The figure of pastoral here is *l'homme moyen sensuel,* whom Butler did in fact idealise with painful results in his own life. Butler's small pet list of endurable artists is interesting because they all did the same trick; it seems clear that he was right in feeling that Handel based himself on ironical humility and used it to reconcile the heroic feelings and the Christian ones.

The man who uses the third sort of comic primness need not, however, go off in these directions; he may simply not be interested in the aspect of the matter that makes it a problem. Aristotle's remarks in the *Rhetoric* about how one should treat evidence extracted by torture, according as it is favourable or not, are a good example, because they show how such a man can seem extremely "innocent" without seeming silly or ill-informed. The question whether it is stupid to torture witnesses at all has obviously occurred to him but is not the matter in hand. Zuckermann's book on Monkey Hill, and much of Darwin for that matter, give the same effect; one sentence may seem Swift satirising Man and the next a scientist satirising scientific method, but the man is keeping himself to one purpose. Even if he is interested in the matter he may imply a claim that it is irrelevant without implying a claim to be ignorant of it. This reserve about the degree to which one has got the matter in hand is of course a central method of irony. And the same effect may be given by someone who has not yet discovered that the problem exists; this may be called "genuine innocence" and in a way returns the third sort of comic primness to the first; the speaker feels that this is a lively way out, the hearer that it is rich in contradictions. This again may be imitated; the ironist may claim that to so good, natural, innocent, etc., a person as himself the problem in hand does not arise—what he says satisfies both parties to the dispute, almost like a pun; there is no way of proving that he is conscious of the problem—if he is made to hear of it he will still feel the same. This is best when so arranged that the other man cannot attempt to call the bluff without exposing himself, which arises naturally in the conventional setting of Comic Primness.

It is obvious that the characters of the *Opera* are in some sense "artificial," though to know just how impossible their talk is one would have to inspect the contemporary Newgate more thoroughly than Gay did or than we can do. (There is a story in *The Flying Post or Weekly Medley*, January 11, 1728–29, to which attention has been drawn recently, showing Gay doing his best to get information from Peachum, but whether it is true or not makes no difference to the argument here.) This feeling of artificiality is, I think, given by the trick essential to mock-pastoral (or the dignity of style which allows of it); we are not enabled to know how much they and how much the author has put into their ironies. The puppets are plausible if they don't mean all that the play puts into their words and delightful if they do, and the shift between the two theories is so easy that we take them as both. One must add doubt about this to the previous doubts about such an irony in plain speech, with which it continually interlocks. To discuss "what the characters mean" is therefore a ridiculous occupation. I shall not, however, guard myself against this mistake; the trick would not work unless the audience was able to imagine for itself a level at which the meanings were just plausible and still delightful, and presumably the author does the same. It is clear, for instance, that Polly's remarks are arranged to fit in with a theory of innocence more than Macheath's, and his again more than Peachum's; Peachum would claim that the problem implied was irrelevant rather than unknown. Indeed the critical attack on"character" in plays previous to the stress on "personality" seems now often pedantic and beyond what a man like Mr. Eliot, who gave the attack its weight, would approve.

> FILCH: Really, madam, I fear I shall be cut off in the
> flower of my youth, so that, every now and again,
> since I was pumped, I have thoughts of taking up
> and going to sea.

The *use* of Filch is that, when you meet young men in other walks of life taking themselves as seriously as he does, you can feel they are like him—unconscious in the way he is. On the other hand (so far as one can separate the feeling of a sentence from the feeling of the whole play), the author means no more by this than to keep up the joke of the style; he does not mean, for instance, that it is always stupid to take oneself seriously. I should call this the Free sort of comic primness in the author, and mere dignity in the speaker.

> MRS. PEACHUM: You should go to Hockley-in-the-Hole,
> and to Marlebone, child, to learn valour; these are
> the schools that have bred so many great men. I
> thought, boy, by this time, thou hadst lost fear as
> well as shame. Poor lad! how little does he know
> yet of the Old Bailey! For the first fact, I'll ensure
> thee against being hanged; and going to sea, Filch,
> will come time enough, upon a sentence of
> transportation. But now, since you have nothing
> better to do, even go to your book, and learn
> your catechism; for, really, a man makes but an ill
> figure in the ordinary's paper who cannot give a
> satisfactory answer to his questions.

"How little he knows yet of life!"—a simple twist localises each sentence to the sort of life considered. To localise so oddly is in itself to generalise—"One would find a prosing and complacent piety as the basis of feeling in any settled way of life." The main thing

the author wants to say is "Take these as ordinary people; there is
nothing queer about them but their economic conditions." Mrs.
Peachum's kind of piety is indeed put in its place, but we are not
told that it need be hypocritical. Yet there seems a touch of archness
in "going to sea, Filch." One can only say that Mrs. Peachum is
between simplicity and the first sort of comic primness, and the author between the first and the third.

> MRS. PEACHUM: How the mother is to be pitied who
>   hath handsome daughters! Locks, bolts, bars, and
>   lectures of morality are nothing to them; they have
>   as much pleasure in cheating a father and mother as
>   in cheating at cards.

(This may look back to the first words of the divine Polly—to
"make a poor hand of her beauty" would be not to cheat with her
cards.) The surprise of the device of rhetoric by which Mrs.
Peachum leaps from the instruments of her trade to a presumption
of virtue makes us feel "all moral lectures are like locks; all used to
imprison others as much as possible." By being a spirited and strik-
ing hypocrite she exposes a normal hypocrisy; the style makes the
critic inherent in the rogue. How far she knows she is amusing for
this reason is a more difficult question; I suppose she has the first
sort of comic primness and the author the third.

> PEACHUM: A lazy dog. . . . This is death, without
>   reprieve. I may venture to book him.

There is a conscious contrast between the decision and the prim
caution about keeping the book neat.

> There is not a fellow that is cleverer in his way, and saves
>   more goods out of the fire, than Ned.

He took advantage of the fire for robbery; "saving is a good act."
Peachum's jokes may well be supposed to be unconscious from
habit, but they imply "these ideas are a bit queer, and allow of lati-
tude, but we have just as much right to them as the others." One
must allow him the third sort of comic primness as well as his author, though the author's hatred of him brings in complications.

   One cannot go far into the play without insisting on the distinction between the two sorts of rogues, which is made very
clearly and gives a rich material for irony. The thieves and whores

parody the aristocratic ideal, the dishonest prison-keeper and thief-catcher and their families parody the bourgeois ideal (though the divine Polly has a foot in both camps); these two ideals are naturally at war, and the rise to power of the bourgeois had made the war important. Their most obvious difference is in the form of Independence that they idealise; thus the Peachums' chief objection to Macheath as a son-in-law is that he is a hanger-on of the aristocracy.

> MRS. PEACHUM: Really, I am sorry, upon Polly's account,
>   the captain hath not more discretion. What business
>   hath he to keep company with lords and gentlemen?
>   He should leave them to prey upon each other.
> PEACHUM: Upon Polly's account? What the plague does
>   the woman mean?

The discovery follows. The puzzle is that both Peachums feel dicing with the aristocracy might involve independence in their sense as well as his.

> MRS. PEACHUM: I knew she was always a proud slut, and
>   now the wench hath played the fool and married,
>   because, forsooth, she would do like the gentry!
>   Can you support the expense of a husband, hussy,
>   in gaming, drinking, and whoring? . . . If you must
>   be married, could you introduce nobody into our
>   family but a highwayman? Why, thou foolish jade,
>   thou wilt be as ill-used and as much neglected as if
>   thou hadst married a lord.
> PEACHUM: Let not your anger, my dear, break through
>   the rules of decency; for the captain looks upon
>   himself in the military capacity as a gentleman by
>   his profession. Besides what he hath already, I
>   know he is in a fair way of getting or dying, and
>   both these, let me tell you, are most excellent
>   chances for a wife. Tell me, hussy, are you ruined
>   or no?
> MRS. PEACHUM: With Polly's fortune she might very well
>   have gone off to a person of distinction; yes, that
>   you might, you pouting slut.

Decency is the polite tone the bourgeois should keep up towards the wasteful aristocrat he half despises, so it is not clear whether *ruined* means "married" or "unmarried"; he is merely, with bourgeois primness, getting the situation clear. But who is a *person of distinction*? Mrs. Peachum is muddled enough to mean a real lord. (First joke; they will marry anything for money.) But she may mean a wealthy merchant or the squire he could become. (Second joke; this gets at the squires by classing them as bourgeois and at the lords by preferring the squires.) Squire Western, a generation later, was indignant in just this way at the idea of marrying his daughter to a lord.

Gay forced this clash onto his material by splitting up the real Jonathan Wild into Peachum and Macheath, who appear in the story as villain and hero. Swift complained that Gay had wasted a chance of good mock-heroic in Macheath's last speech to the gang; he should have said "let my empire be to the worthiest" like Alexander. Gay was busy with his real feelings, and Macheath says, "Bring those villains to the gallows before you, and I am satisfied." But though he hates Peachum he makes him the parody of a real sort of dignity, that of the man making an independent income in his own line of business, and seems to have been puzzled between the two ideals in his own life. In the play the conflict is hardly made real except in the character of Polly; the fact that both parties are compared to Walpole serves to weaken it to the tone of comedy.

The ironies of the two parties are naturally of different intentions.

> JEMMY: . . . Why are the laws levelled at us? Are we
> more dishonest than the rest of mankind? What we
> win, gentlemen, is our own, by the law of arms
> and the right of conquest.
> [This specially heroic member peached.]
> CROOK: Where shall we find such another set of practical
> philosophers, who, to a man, are above the fear of
> death?
> WAT: Sound men, and true.
> ROBIN: Of tried courage, and indefatigable industry.
> NED: Who is there here that would not die for his friend?
> HARRY: Who is there here that would betray him for his
> interest?
> MAT: Show me a gang of courtiers that can say as much.
> BEN: We are for a just partition of the world, for every
> man hath a right to enjoy life.

The main effect of this mutual comparison, of the assumption of a heroic manner here, is to make the aristocrats seem wicked and the thieves vain. But even for this purpose it must act the other way, and make both charming by exchanging their virtues; that the aristocrats can be satirised like this partly justifies the thieves, and to extend to Walpole's government the sort of sympathy it was generous to feel for the thieves was strong satire precisely because it was gay. The author means the passage hardly less than the thieves do as a statement of an attitude admittedly heroic; Ben Budge anticipates Jefferson, and the whole complaint against the morality of the play was that they are too hard to answer. No doubt there is a further critical irony in the author—"the whole business of admiring Marlborough and Alexander is nonsense"; and in people like thieves, in whom heroism does so much less harm than politicians, Gay is ready enough for an irresponsible sort of admiration. It seems enough, if one requires a tidy formula, to say that the thieves have both grandeur and the first sort of comic primness and their author the third.

The political ironies of Peachum and Lockit are of a different sort. The difficulty in saying whether they mean their ironies does not arise because they are simpleminded but because they are indifferent; they bring out the justification that they are necessary to the state and partake of its dignity firmly and steadily, as a habitual politeness, and this goes on till we see them as portentous figures with the whole idea of the state, sometimes a cloud that's dragonish, dissolving in their hands.

> PEACHUM: In one respect indeed we may be reckoned
>   dishonest, because, like great statesmen, we
>   encourage those who betray their friends.
> LOCKIT: Such language, brother, anywhere else might
>   turn to your prejudice. Learn to be more guarded, I
>   beg you.

Either "it is not safe to accuse the great" or "it is bad for any man's credit to admit that in anything he is as bad as they are." But there is no sense of surprise in this double meaning; the primness of caution is merely indistinguishable from the primness of superior virtue.

> PEACHUM: 'Tis for our mutual interest, 'tis for the
>   interest of the world that we should agree. If I said

> anything, brother, to the prejudice of your credit, I
> ask pardon.

Credit is used both about business and glory—"that fellow, though he were to live these six months, will never come to the gallows with any credit." *The world* may be the whole of society or Society, the only people who are "anybody," the rich who alone receive the benefits of civilisation. The traditional hero has a magical effect on everything; the Whig politicians act like tradesmen but affect the whole country; Lockit and Peachum have the heroic dignity of the great because they too have a calculating indifference to other men's lives. The point of the joke is that the villains are right, not that they are wrong; "the root of the normal order of society is a mean injustice; it is ludicrous to be complacent about this; but one cannot conceive its being otherwise." The conclusion is not that society should be altered but that only the individual can be admired.

This double-irony method, out of which the jokes are constructed, is inherent in the whole movement of the story. We feel that Macheath's death is not "downright deep tragedy," nor his reprieve—a sort of insult to the audience not made real in the world of the play—a happy ending, because, after all, the characters, from their extraordinary way of life, are all going to die soon anyway; then this turns back and we feel that we are all going to die soon anyway. One of the splendid plain phrases of Macheath brings out the feeling very sharply:

> A moment of time may make us unhappy for ever.

The antithesis might make *for ever* "in the life of eternity" from a speaker who expected such a thing, or as derived from heaven "in one of those moments whose value seems outside time." His life seems the more dazzlingly brief because "for ever" assumes it is unending.

> That Jemmy Twitcher should peach me I own surprised
> me. 'Tis a plain proof that the world is all alike, and that
> even our gang can no more trust one another than other
> people; therefore, I beg you, gentlemen, to look well to
> yourselves, for, in all probability, you may live some
> months longer.

"And no more; take care because you are in danger" is the plain sense; but the turn of the phrase suggests "You may live as long as several months, so it is worth taking trouble. If you were dying soon like me you might be at peace." It is by these faint double meanings that he gets genuine dignity out of his ironical and genteel calm.

An odd trick is used to drive this home; as most literature uses the idea of our eventual death as a sort of frame or test for its conception of happiness, so this play uses hanging.

> LUCY: How happy am I, if you say this from your heart!
> For I love thee so, that I could sooner bear to see
> thee hanged than in the arms of another.

It is true enough, but she means merely "dead" by *hanged;* no other form of death occurs to her.

> MRS. PEACHUM: Away, hussy. Hang your husband, and
> be dutiful.

Hang here has its real sense crossed with the light use in swearing— "don't trouble about him; he's a nuisance; be dutiful to your parents."

> POLLY: And will absence change your love?
> MACHEATH: If you doubt it, let me stay—and be hanged.

"Whatever happens" or even "and be hanged to you," but he really would be hanged.

> MACHEATH (in prison): To what a woeful plight have I
> brought myself! Here must I (all day long, till I am
> hanged) be confined to hear the reproaches of a
> wench who lays her ruin at my door.

His natural courage, and the joke that the scolding woman is a terror to which all others are as nothing, give "till I am hanged" the force of "for the rest of my life," as if he was merely married to her. Finally as a clear light use:

> PEACHUM: Come home, you slut, and when your fellow
> is hanged, hang yourself, to make your family some
> amends.

Hanging in the songs may even become a sort of covert metaphor for true love. "Oh twist thy fetters about me, that he may not haul me from thee," cries Polly very gracefully, but her song while her father is hauling carries a different suggestion.

> No power on earth can e'er divide
> The knot that sacred love hath joined.
> When parents draw against our mind
> The true love's knot they faster bind.

It is the hangman's knot, and the irony goes on echoing through the play. The songs can afford to be metaphysical poetry in spite of their date because they are intended to be comically "low"; only an age of reason could put so much beauty into burlesque or would feel it needed the protection; they take on the vigour of thought which does not fear to be absurd. This excellence depends on the same ironical generosity—a feeling that life is fresh among these people—as lies behind Gay's whole attitude to his characters. (The point that genuine pastoral could then only be reached through burlesque was indeed made clearly by Johnson about Gay's own admirable *Pastorals*.)

There are two elements in the joke of this. One comes from the use of the local details of a special way of life for poetry regardless of how they seem to outsiders, like Johnson's *Rambler* showing how an Esquimau would take metaphors for his love-rhetoric from seal blubber. This in itself is satisfying to the age of reason because it shows the universal forces at work. Secondly it uses the connection between death (here hanging) and the sexual act, which is not merely a favourite of Freud but a common joke of the period; the first effect of this is to give an odd ironical courage to the wit of the characters.

> Here ends all dispute, for the rest of our lives,
> For this way, at once, I please all my wives.
> Which way shall I turn me, how can I decide?
> Wives, the day of our death, are as fond as a bride.

The joke need not be given the additional deathliness of the joke against marriage:

> MRS. TRAPES: If you have blacks of any kind, brought in
> of late, mantoes, velvet scarfs, petticoats, let it be
> what you will, I am your chap, for all my ladies are
> very fond of mourning.

Both the ladies want to be hanged "with" Macheath, in the supreme song of the play; "*but* hark," he replies, there is the bell; this is real death, which one dies alone.

A song by Mrs. Peachum, that lady of easy sentiment, introduced early to make us clear on the point, shows the range of ideas
in this direct and casual comedy.

> If any wench Venus' girdle wear,
> Though she be never so ugly,
> Lilies and roses will quickly appear,
> And her face look wondrous smugly.

A rich irony identifies the beauty created by desire in the eye of the
beholder with self-satisfaction. The last word admits and enjoys the
banality of the preceding flower symbols.

> Behind the left ear so fit but a cord
> (A rope so charming a zone is!)

Monks use them as zones; they stand for asceticism.

> The youth in his cart hath the air of a lord,

Macheath is a "captain"; it is the military hero's chariot of triumph.
(When the cart is driven away he is left hanging.)

> And we cry, There dies an Adonis!

> —Whose annual wound in Lebanon allured
> The Syrian damsels to lament his fate
> In amorous ditties all a summer's day

—whose tragic sacrifice, every spring, like Christ, makes the crops
grow. It is a rare case of the full use of the myth.

At Mrs. Peachum's first entry she finds her husband deciding
which thief to hang next sessions; her cue is the end of the laugh at
a string of aliases for Walpole.

> MRS. PEACHUM: What of Bob Booty, husband? I hope
> nothing bad hath betided him. You know, my dear,
> he's a favourite customer of mine—'twas he, made
> me a present of this ring.
> PEACHUM: I have set his name down in the black list,
> that's all, my dear; he spends his life among
> women, and, as soon as his money is gone, one or
> other of the ladies will hang him for the reward,
> and there's forty pound lost to us for ever!
> MRS. PEACHUM: You know, my dear, I never meddle in
> matters of death; I always leave those affairs to you.

> Women, indeed, are bitter bad judges in these cases;
> for they are so partial to the brave, that they think
> every man handsome who is going to the camp, or
> the gallows.

The song follows. "Spends his life among women" means among prostitutes; not to say so implies that they are what all women are. Mrs. P.'s callous squeamishness only points the moral; the reason that all women are bitter bad judges about killing men by treachery is that they find so much interest in doing it to their lovers. It is the first hint of that eerie insistence on the sex war by which the play makes betrayal itself a lascivious act.

Perhaps the most grisly version of this notion is the one relapse into sentiment of the great Peachum. By this time Mrs. Peachum (who pleaded for a brave man before) is firmly entrenched in brutality behind her bourgeois "duty."

> MRS. PEACHUM, PEACHUM, POLLY listening.
> MRS. PEACHUM: The thing, husband, must and shall be
> done. For the sake of intelligence we must take
> other measures and have him peached the next
> session without her consent. If she will not know
> her duty we know ours.
> PEACHUM: But, really, my dear! it grieves one's heart to
> take off a great man. When I consider his personal
> bravery, his fine stratagems, how much we have
> already got by him, and how much more we may
> get, methinks I can't find it in my heart to have a
> hand in his death: I wish you could have made
> Polly undertake it.
> MRS. PEACHUM: But in a case of necessity—our own lives
> are in danger.
> PEACHUM: Then indeed we must comply with the
> customs of the world, and make gratitude give way
> to interest.

Then indeed—when not heroic one can always be sure to be respectable, because bourgeois, because self-seeking. She started with the insinuating pomp of the language of diplomacy. Their lives are in no danger; they only think Macheath will betray them because they think he is like Peachum. To be heroic would be to hang on for what they can get. Warmed into feelings of generosity by this situation, and fretfully wishing that Polly might save him the moral effect of deciding to violate them, he shows a fleeting sympathy with romantic love, which so often kills its loved one, and of which at other times, in his bourgeois virtue, he disapproves. Swift is beaten clean off the field here.

The same idea is implicit in one of the purest of Polly's fancies.

> LUCY, MACHEATH, POLLY. (The condemned Hold.)
> POLLY (entering): Where is my dear husband? Was ever a
> rope intended for this neck! Oh, let me throw my
> arms about it, and throttle thee with love. . . .
> What means my love? not one kind word! not one
> kind look! Think what thy Polly suffers to see thee
> in this condition!

> Thus when the swallow, seeking prey,
>   Within the sash is closely pent,
> His consort with bemoaning lay
>   Without sits pining for the event.
> Her chattering lovers round her skim;
> She heeds them not, poor bird, her soul's with him.

Her first words say that her love is death; her love has caused his arrest; the presence of her love here only makes it impossible for him to be saved by the love of Lucy. "Think what your Polly suffers"; even without these accidents her love would be mere additional torture. And for what *event* is the consort (which also seeks *prey*) of this swallow *pining*? *Event* may mean "whatever happens," but the sense thrown at us is "the thing happening," the exciting thing; they both mean to be in at the death.

> LUCY: Am I then bilked of my virtue?

"The thing I have *paid* for?"—the slang verb drags in a ludicrous and frightfully irrelevant bit of money-satire. Only the unyielding courage of Macheath, who keeps the thing firmly on the level of the obvious, gives one the strength to take it as comedy or even to feel the pathos of the appeal of Polly.

> LUCY: Hadst thou been hanged five months ago, I had
> been happy.
> POLLY: And I too. If you had been kind to me till death,
> it would not have vexed me—and that's no very
> unreasonable request (though from a wife) to a man
> who hath not above seven or eight days to live.

He takes so completely for granted their state of self-centredness tempered by bloodlust that the main overtone of her speech is that so often important to the play—"we have all very few days to live, and must live with spirit." The selfishness of her remarks reconciles us to his selfish treatment of her, and the idea behind their pathos to his way of life.

So that to follow up the ideas of "love-betrayal-death," the sacred delight in the tragedy of the hero, is to reach those of "pathetic right to selfishness," the ideal of Independence. This comes out more clearly in the grand betrayal scene of the second act, of Macheath by the prostitutes. The climax is one of the double ironies.

> JENNY: These are the tools of a man of honour. Cards
> and dice are only fit for cowardly cheats, who prey
> on their friends.
> (*She takes up the pistol; Tawdry takes up the other.*)

(First laugh; the great are like the rogues but more despicable.) Having got his pistols she calls in the police. (Second laugh; the rogues are after all as despicable as the great.) But this is not merely a trick of surprise because she means it; "we are better than the others only because we know the truth about all human beings"; the characters are always making this generalisation. "Of all beasts of prey," remarks Lockit, "mankind is the only sociable one." The play only defends its characters by making them seem the norm of mankind and its most informed critics, and does this chiefly by the time interval in their ironies.

> JENNY: I must and will have a kiss to give my wine a
> zest.
> (*They take him about the neck, and make signs to the
> constables, who rush in upon him.*)
> PEACHUM: I seize you, sir, as my prisoner.

It is the kiss of Judas, an expression of love with a parallel to hanging in it, like Polly's, that gives zest. Wine is normally used as a symbol of spiritual intoxication, but in this play the spirit is a sinister one, rather as the word *pleasure,* which it uses continually, always refers to the pleasures ("mystical" because connected with death wishes) of cheating, or cruelty, or death. The five other uses, counting *pleased,* that I don't quote, are all of this sort. The doubtful one is Lockit's—

Bring us then more liquor. To-day shall be for pleasure,
to-morrow for business.

He has told the audience that he will make Peachum drunk and so
have the pleasure of cheating him.

The more sinister because by making the pleasure of betrayal a
mere condiment she claims that to her the affair is trivial—"What
you can be made to feel heartbreaking I have the strength to judge
rightly." Anyway the *zest* keeps us from thinking her so stupid as
to be mercenary about it, which would be to feel nothing.

Peachum treats Macheath here with a sinister respect not
chiefly intended as mockery; all politeness has an element of irony,
but this is a recognition of the captain's claims; he is now half divine because fated to sacrifice.

> PEACHUM: You must now, sir, take your leave of the
> ladies; and, if they have a mind to make you a visit,
> they will be sure to find you at home [and sure of
> the "last pleasure" of seeing the execution. The
> preliminaries of death are a failure in the sex war,
> since the ladies can no longer be deceived, even if
> death itself is a triumph in it]. The gentleman,
> ladies, lodges in Newgate. Constables, wait upon
> the captain to his lodgings.

> MACHEATH: At the tree I shall suffer with pleasure,
> At the tree I shall suffer with pleasure;
> > Let me go where I will
> > In all kinds of ill
> I shall find no such furies as these are.

He can't go where he will—he expects to leave prison only for
Hell. The half-poetical, half-slang word *tree* applies both to the gib-
bet and to the cross, where the supreme sacrificial hero suffered,
with ecstasy.

> PEACHUM: Ladies, I'll take care the reckoning shall be
> discharged.
> (*Exit Macheath, guarded, with Peachum and constables.*)

He, not they, is the fury, the avenging snake goddess; to look after
the reckoning is his whole function towards both parties. The delicacy of his irony (this, I think, is a rule about good ironies) is that

it can safely leave you guessing about both parties' consciousness of it; the more sincerely he treats Macheath as an aristocrat the more cruelly he isolates him—

> (*In the condemned Hold.*)
>
> LOCKIT: Do but examine them, sir—never was better
> work—how genteelly they are made. They will fit
> as easily as a glove, and the nicest gentleman in
> England *might* not be ashamed to wear them. (He
> puts on the chains.) If I had the best gentleman in
> the land in my custody, I could not equip him more
> handsomely. And so, sir, I now leave you to your
> private meditations.

—the less sincerely, the more he mocks—but at the whole notion of aristocracy that Macheath has aped into disaster. Thus even if the insincerity was expressed grossly, so that Macheath could appeal through it to his audience ("obviously you mean this, and it is unfair") he could still not appeal against it as a personal insult ("I really *have* the virtues of the aristocrat"); they would then be mocked, and he would have confessed he was not one of them. Such an irony is a sort of intellectual imitation of more valuable states of mind. To the opponent, there is no practical use in distinguishing between whether the man is conscious or unconscious of his meaning—if he isn't he will be when he is told. "Oh, so you thought that funny, did you? Well, I wasn't thinking of that special case, but it seems to apply to that all right." The force of irony is its claim to innocence; the reason for its wide usefulness is that the claim may still be plausible when the man's consciousness of his irony is frank—"This is the normal thing to feel; I felt this before I had met people like you."

Overpoliteness is a form of comic primness worth looking at for a moment in general. The original sense is "I respect you too much to be less formal," and the effect is to shut you out from intimacy; "I want you to be formal too." This may be a coy claim to attention, since to be shut out suggests a desire to come in, or an insult, since you may be below the intimacy not above it. The combination says, "Notice that I would like to insult you but will not grant you even that form of intimacy." However, the politeness accepts you as a civilised person, since otherwise it would be no use; "You ought to know already that we can't be intimate." This also allows of irony: "I am polite on principle even to people like you; the best people do this, because any one may deserve it; but it is curious to reflect that even you may." And it may show that it is not trying to hide these meanings or that it thinks you too much of a fool to see them. The last, I think, is what makes Pope's *Epistle to Augustus* so peculiarly insulting: "I am safe in saying this, though you would persecute me if you could understand it, because you can't."

I must go back to the betrayal scene.

> MACHEATH: Was this well done, Jenny? Women are
> decoy ducks, who can trust them? Beasts, jades,
> jilts, harpies, furies, whores.

He may mean that these women are whores, which is no discovery, or that all women are, which is made plausible only by being half-said. The climax, the worst he can say of them, is the obvious, which brings back a sort of comedy to the strain of the scene. But its trenchant flatness also makes us feel that the second meaning is obvious, though it would contradict the first (he could not blame them for being like everybody). Even this is a sort of double irony.

"Was this well done?" belongs to Cleopatra in all the versions of her story. It does not matter whether we take Macheath as quoting it (he quotes Shakespeare a moment before) or reinventing it, but it would be wrong to take it only as a comic misuse of heroic dignity like Ancient Pistol's; however queer the logic may be there should be a grand echo in one's mind from the reply of Charmian:

> It is well done, and fitting for a princess
> Descended from so many mighty kings.

—indeed Peachum drives the point home at once:

> Your case, Mr. Macheath, is not particular; the greatest
> heroes have been undone by women.

The pleasure in seeing that two systems so different to emotion or morality as Antony and Macheath work in the same way is connected with the Royal Society, but there are queerer forces in it than that.

Grand only by simplicity and concentration, and only by this grandeur not normal colloquial English (so that it is a reliable phrase for Macheath), the question owes its tenseness to its peculiar assumptions; if it is fitting the other person must have thought the act good, not merely allowable, and yet must be capable of being made to see that it is wrong by a mere appeal. So there must be a powerful and obvious clash of two modes of judgment. When it is used to Cleopatra one must remember that by choosing this death she destroys her children only to avoid a hurt to her pride (not till her being carted in the triumph becomes certain does the world become empty for her without Antony); that the soldier who speaks feels that she has broken her word to Caesar; that Shakespeare's play has made us suspect her of planning to betray Antony, and that some of her tantrums—dragging the messenger about by the hair—can only have seemed comic, vulgar and wicked. Only by a magnificent forcing of the sympathies of the audience is she made a tragic figure in the last act. The sentence, then, used to her, means "You have cheated Caesar and destroyed yourself; you think this heroic but it is childish; it is like the way you cheated Antony till you destroyed him." It is because of this suggestion that the answer of Charmian seems to call back and justify Cleopatra's whole life; all her acts were indeed like this one; all therefore fitting for a princess. It is a measure of the queerness of this alarming tragedy (no one can say how much irony there is in the barge speech) that the effect of the question is very little altered when it is "parodied" for the comic opera; both uses give a quasi-mystical "justification by death" which does not pretend to justify by normal standards.

So to explain the effect of the phrase here (it is a great effect) one has to invent queer but plausible reasons for thinking "This was well done." The most obvious is that the betrayal is poetic justice on him for being unfaithful to Polly; the structure of the play indeed insists on this. The first act gives the personal situation; we meet Polly, her parents at their business, finally Macheath, secretly married to her and hiding in the house. From his richly prepared entry to the end of the first act he goes on swearing eternal faithfulness to her—"if you doubt it, let me stay—and be hanged." Two grand scenes of the second act then introduce us to the tribe of which these two are symbolic heroes, the society of which they are flowers (for Polly, unlike her parents, is "aristocratic" as well as "bourgeois")—to the eight thieves of Macheath's gang, which he dare not join since Polly's father is now his enemy, then to the eight whores he collects because he must be idle.

> I must have women—there is nothing unbends the mind
> like them; money is not so strong a cordial for the time.

Cordial, medicine for the heart, implies drink, which gives courage—love is an intoxication. To unbend your mind is to loosen the
strong bow of your thought so that it will be strong in the next
demand on it; a statesman's excuse for pleasure (indeed *the time*
seems to imply "this unfortunate but no doubt brief period of history"); used here with a ludicrous or pathetic dignity whose very
untruth has the gay dignity of intentional satire. Macheath, like Antony, like the ambitious politician, must unbend his mind because
he must forget his fears. Into his statement of this fact, whose confession of fear frees it from bravado, he throws a further comparison to the avarice inherent in the life of safety he despises (so that
these few words include both bourgeois and aristocrat); "to those
who live within the law the mere possession of money is a sufficient intoxication." But however well he talks he is treating Polly
with contempt:

> What a fool is a fond wench! Polly is most confoundedly
> bit. I love the sex; and a man who loves money might as
> well be contented with one guinea, as I with one woman.

(Satire on money justifies anything.)

> Do all we can, women will believe us; for they look upon
> a promise as an excuse for following their own inclin-
> ations.

("However frankly theatrical we make our professions of heroic
love, professions which necessarily have the irony inherent in all
fixed rules of politeness, such as are essential to civilisation.") It was
the innocence and pathos of Polly in "oh ponder well," we are told,
that swung round the audience on the first night. From the stand-
point of heroic love the act was well done.

In any case the woman who really undoes him is not Jenny but
Polly, however much against her will; unselfish love leads to honest
marriage, and therefore Polly's father is determined to have him
killed. It is love at its best that is the most fatal. This forces her to
be like Cleopatra, and may make it poetic justice that he should betray her; anyway it removes much of the guilt from Jenny. And

there is always, since this brings the thing nearer to a stock tragedy, the idea that it is in a fundamental way "well done" to cause the hero's death because it is necessary to the play.

But there is a more curious pathos in the question if one forgets about Polly, as Macheath has done. It is the questioner here who has both answers to the question in his mind. The "compliments" of the ladies to one another, through which he has sat placidly drinking, treat just such betrayals by Jenny only as acts of heroic self-control.

> MRS. COAXER: If any woman hath more art than another,
> to be sure 'tis Jenny Diver. Though her fellow be
> never so agreeable, she can pick his pocket as coolly
> as if money were her only pleasure. Now that is a
> command of the passions uncommon in a woman.
> JENNY: I never go to a tavern with a man but in the way
> of business. I have other hours, and other sort of
> men, for my pleasure. But had I your address,
> madam—

(On the face of things a prostitute is unlike other women in only wanting money. In this satire a prostitute is an independent woman who wants all the nobility included in the idea of freedom, and a chaste genteel woman only wants a rich marriage. If you hate Jenny for betraying the hero then she is actually as bad as a good woman, but Mrs. Coaxer assumes that she obviously can't be, and therefore that her behaviour on the crucial issue of money shows nobility; she is faithful to her sorority when she acts like this. Jenny's reply shows the humility of a truly heroic soul.)

> MACHEATH: Have done with your compliments, ladies,
> and drink about. You are not so fond of me, Jenny,
> as you used to be.
> JENNY: 'Tis not convenient, sir, to show my fondness
> before so many rivals. 'Tis your own choice, and
> not my inclination, that will determine you.

He cannot say she has deceived him. "What," he says as she enters:

> And my pretty Jenny Diver too! as prim and demure as
> ever! There is not any prude, however high bred, hath a
> more sanctified look, with a more mischievous heart: ah,
> thou art a dear artful hypocrite!

He loves her for having the power to act as she so soon acts to him (there is a bitter gentility in it which he too feels to be heroic) both as a walking satire on the claims to delicacy of the fine ladies and as justified in her way of life by her likeness to the fine ladies, whose superiority he half admits.

> MACHEATH: . . . If any of the ladies choose gin, I hope
> they will be so free as to call for it.
> JENNY: You look as if you meant me. Wine is strong
> enough for me. Indeed, sir, I never drink strong
> waters but when I have the colic.
> MACHEATH: Just the excuse of the fine ladies! why, a lady
> of quality is never without the colic.

The colic as a justification for drinking is a disease like the spleen, half-mental, caused by a life of extreme refinement, especially as expressed by tight-lacing. It is because he so fully understands and appreciates her half-absurd charm that he is so deeply shocked by what should have been obvious, that it is a weapon frankly used against himself.

His respect for her is very near the general respect for independence; the main conflict in his question is that between individualism and the need for loyalty. In being a "beast of prey," the play repeats, she is like all humanity except in her self-knowledge and candour, which make her better. She is the test and therefore somehow the sacrifice of her philosophy; quasi-heroic because she takes a theory to its extreme; if wrong then because she was "loyal" to it. Macheath's question becomes "It is a fine thing when individuals like us can sustain themselves against society. But for that very reason we ought to hold together; surely it is not well done of you to prey upon *me*"—with the idea "I thought I could make her love me so much that I could disarm her." Jenny's answer is supplied by Mrs. Slammekin in her complaint at not sharing in the profits; "I think Mr. Peachum, after so long an acquaintance, might have trusted me as well as Jenny Diver"; she owes as much faith to the professional betrayer as to Macheath in his capacity of genteel rake, "martyr to the fair."

But Macheath does not believe in individualism in this sense; honour among thieves is taken for granted and only a boast by contrast with politicians. He believes his second arrest to be due to Jemmy Twitcher, and this seems really to shock him. The question does not simply mean (what is inherent in it) "we believe in all against all, but now I am horrified by it." It is only in matters of love that he has so nearly believed in all against all as to put a real shock into the question. He has really a sort of love for her (partly because she is against all). He has of course treated her with more contempt than Polly. So that the more serious you make their feelings for each other the more strongly you invoke the other notion, which applies also to Polly; not Independence but Love-Betrayal-Death; "it is especially in all lovers that we see that all human beings, being independent, are forced to prey upon one another."

These notions must now be pursued into the character of Polly, where their irony is more subtle. She has been idealised ever since her first night. In the self-righteous sequel named after her, when they are all transported, Gay made Macheath a weak fish permanently in the clutches of Jenny Diver and Polly the only civilised character able to sustain the high tone demanded by the Noble Savage. Her first words in the play [*The Beggar's Opera*], at an entry for which our curiosity has been worked up for two and a half pages, make a rather different impression. She uses the same comic primness as her father and his clients—a friend of Richardson's told him he was too fond of "tarantalising" like Polly—and this delicate device in a dramatist may wish one to feel any shade of sympathy toward the speaker. You may say that this is a bold and subtle trick to defeat the tone of the play and bring on a real good heroine (if she is not careful she will seem a prig), or that she is defending her lover by a process unusual to her; so that the audience will have a pleasant surprise on discovering her true character. There is more in it than that.

> POLLY: I know as well as any of the fine ladies how to
> make the most of myself and of my man too. A
> woman knows how to be mercenary, though she
> hath never been in a court or at an assembly. We
> have it in our natures, papa. If I allow Captain
> Macheath some trifling liberties, I have this watch
> and other visible marks of his favour to show for it.
> A girl who cannot grant some things, and refuse
> what is most material, will make a poor hand of her
> beauty, and soon be thrown upon the common.

(The common is the heath that her husband rules.)

This might be an attack on her under both heads, as making a false fine-lady claim and having real shopkeeper vices. She has two songs, and there are near two pages, containing the discovery that she is married, before she can safely be let speak again.

Peachum's remarks about her do not make up our minds for us—

> If the girl had the discretion of a court lady, who can have a dozen young fellows at her ear without complying with one, I should not matter it.

It is her innocence, which he admits, that is untrustworthy; it is a form of sensuality; especially because certain to change.

She does not say what is "most material," either from the modesty of virtue, the slyness of evil, or the necessity of deceiving her father; her real object may be to reform Macheath and make him an honest shopkeeper. One may take either way her classing the unmentioned marriage lines with the flaunted watch, and the dignity of its appearance among general terms may be pathetic from avarice or from a simple pride. "*We* have it in our natures, papa," either because theft is in our blood, or because our nature is to be intelligent as well as good, and could not reliably be good otherwise. This is an early example of the joke from comic primness about the innocent young girl, which runs on through Sheridan, Thackeray, Dodgson, and Wilde—that it is only proper for her to be worldly, because she, like the world, should know the value of her condition, and that there must be no question of whether she is conscious or not of being worldly, so that she is safe (much too safe) from your calling the bluff of her irony, because she deserves either not to be told of the cold judgments of the world or not to be reminded of them. "Make the most of my man" may mean "make the most money possible out of the man I am working on now" or "have the best influence I can on this man to whom my life is now bound"; nor would it be graceful in her to claim that the second is wholly unselfish and so distinguish it from the first. If she is able to deceive her father by this phrase it is a perquisite rightly due to the language of delicacy and understanding. Yet on the highest view of her she is absurd; what could any woman "make" of Macheath, already a limited perfection? To make him honest would be to make him mercenary. She might indeed (I suspect Gay ran away from this very ironical theme in *Polly*) make him a Virginian squire after transportation, as Moll Flanders did her "very fine gentleman, as he really is." The exquisite sense of freedom in one of the ballad lines used by the songs—"over the hills and far away"—is twisted into a romantic view of transportation by a remark of Polly just before. But she doesn't see her way to that now; she is not so placed as to have one purpose and one meaning.

Indeed the fascination of the character is that one has no means of telling whether she is simple or ironical; not merely because if ironical she would speak as if simple, but because if simple it would be no shock to her, it would be a mere shift of the conscious focus, to be told her meanings if ironical. The effect is that "the contradictions do not arise for her; she is less impeded than we are." This sort of thing usually requires complacence, and the Victorians did it very well, as in the mellowness of the jumps from spirituality to intrigue in Trollope's clerical death scenes. Polly accepts her parents' wise advice, though she cannot live up to it, as readily as their high moral tone, as readily as she makes herself useful by telling lies to their customers; that she is so businesslike makes us believe in the vigour of her goodness; "real goodness knows that if its practice in an imperfect world is to be for the best its acts must be imperfect." She grants fully that her love is a weakness; her excuse for marriage even in a song has a delicate reserve in its double use of the inevitable criteria:

> I thought it both safest and best

is as near as a lyric will carry her to a moral claim. You may always think her as bad as they are. Her most shocking effects of pathos, like the play's best jokes, come from a firm acceptance of her parents' standards, which gives her the excuse always needed by poetry for a flat statement of the obvious. Circumstances make the low seem to her the normal, so she can use without affectation the inverted hypocrisy of Swift.

> PEACHUM: And had you not the common views of a
>   gentlewoman in your marriage, Polly?
> POLLY: I don't know what you mean, sir.
> PEACHUM: Of a jointure, and of being a widow. . . .
>   Since the thing sooner or later must happen, I
>   daresay the captain himself would like that we
>   should get the reward for his death sooner than a
>   stranger. . . .

> MRS. PEACHUM: But your duty to your parents, hussy,
> obliges you to hang him. What would many a wife
> give for such an opportunity!
> POLLY: What is a jointure, what is widowhood, to me? I
> know my heart, I cannot survive him.

No less rich background of irony would let us feel that this was true, and a discovery, and a confession, and yet not be too burlesque for us to feel seriously about her.

> MRS. PEACHUM: What! is the wench in love in earnest
> then? I hate thee for being particular. Why, wench,
> thou art a shame to thy sex.
> POLLY: But, hear me, mother—if you ever loved—
> MRS. PEACHUM: These cursed playbooks she reads have
> been her ruin. One word more, hussy, and I shall
> knock your brains out, if you have any.

This playbook itself, as the moralists insisted, is as likely as the others, like them through its very idealism, to bring ruin. Mrs. Peachum does well to be angry and is right in her suspicion ("I find in the romance you lent me, that none of the great heroes was ever false in love"). But the objection to love is not merely that of Puritan virtue or bourgeois caution; independence is involved. Because love puts this supreme virtue in danger good faith is there most of all necessary, but because of "love-betrayal-death" is there least obtained. A still more searching point is made in dealing with the weaker and more violent Lucy.

> LOCKIT: And so you have let him escape, hussy—have
> you?
> LUCY: When a woman loves, a kind word, a tender
> look, can persuade her to anything, and I could ask
> no other bribe. [Love is a form of money, as
> contemptible and as easy to cheat with as another.]
> LOCKIT: Thou wilt always be a vulgar slut, Lucy. If you
> would not be looked upon as a fool, you should
> never do anything but upon the foot of interest.
> Those that act otherwise are their own bubbles.
> LUCY: But love, sir, is a misfortune that may happen to
> the most discreet woman, and in love we are all
> fools alike. Notwithstanding all that he swore, I am
> now fully convinced that Polly Peachum is actually

> his wife. Did I let him escape, fool that I was! to go
> to her? Polly will wheedle herself into his money;
> and then Peachum will hang him, and cheat us
> both.

One might think Independence a brutish ideal imposed by a false intellectualism. Lockit makes it a polite social trick, a decent hiding of the reality, to pretend that one is a beast of prey. It is from a social criterion that Lucy is told to be antisocial and not "vulgar." You may call this an admission that the ideal, as a defence of selfishness, does not meet the facts of human nature; the joke is that as a cynicism the thing refutes itself; but there is a joke too against Lockit and the conventions. We are left with an acceptance of Egoist ethical theory. And the philosophical joke fits naturally onto the social one; only the rogue or the aristocrat, only the independent character, can afford to see the truth about the matter.

We return here to the Senecan remark of Lockit: "Of all beasts of prey, mankind is the only sociable one." The reason for the breadth of this remark, its wide use for a cult of independence, is that it gives two contradictory adjectives to man. One cannot reduce it to a gangster blow-the-gaff sentiment, implying "see how tough I am." In the first place it may involve an appeal to individualist theory—"all actions apparently altruistic must have a solid basis in the impulses of the individual, and only so can be understood. They can only be based on self-love, because the individual is alone; there is merely nothing else for them to be based on. Only by facing this, by understanding the needs of the individual, can society be made safe." Secondly there is a more touching and less analytic idea—"all life is too painful for the impulses of altruism to be possible. To refuse to accept this is to judge your fellow creatures unjustly." That man should be made unique in this way is indeed a boast about his reason and the power that it gives to be independent; all the ramifications of irony that drive home and generalise this idea relate it to the central cult of the man who can stand alone. Of course the claim to be such a man is as pathetic in a Restoration thief as a Chicago tough, but the play makes us feel that.

For there is no doubt about the sociability. One of the most terrible of these comic scenes is that between Lucy and Polly, one attempting murder, the other suspecting it, and yet each finding "comfort" in each other's company. The play has made the word ready for them to wring the last ironies from it.

PEACHUM: But make haste to Newgate, boy, and let my
friends know what I intend; for I love to make
them easy, one way or the other.

FILCH: When a gentleman is long kept in suspense,
penitence may break his spirit ever after. Besides,
certainty gives a man a good air upon his trial, and
makes him risk another without fear or scruple. But
I'll away, for 'tis a pleasure to be a messenger of
comfort to friends in affliction.

Death is the comfort, for most, and it is a pleasure to tell them of
it. Polly tells her mother she has married for love; she faints, thinking the girl had been better bred:

PEACHUM: See, wench, to what a condition you have
reduced your poor mother! A glass of cordial this
instant! How the poor woman takes it to heart!
[POLLY goes out, and returns with it.]
Ah hussy, now this is the only comfort your
mother has left.

POLLY: Give her another glass, sir; my mother drinks
double the quantity whenever she is out of order.

When she isn't, it is still her chief comfort. All this leads up to
Lucy's great scene.

LUCY: . . . I have the ratsbane ready—I run no risk; for I
can lay her death upon the gin, and so many die of
that naturally, that I shall never be called in
question. But say I were to be hanged—I never
could be hanged for anything that would give me
greater comfort than the poisoning that slut.

Death is certain anyhow, and its name is hanging throughout the
play.

[Enter POLLY.]
. . . Dear madam, your servant. I hope you will
pardon my passion when I was so happy to see you
last—I was so overrun with the spleen, that I was
perfectly out of myself; and really when one hath
the spleen, everything is to be excused by a friend.

The spleen is aristocratic, so her use of poison is also to be excused. Their faults are always the result of their greatness of soul.

> LUCY: When a wife's in her pout
>   (As she's sometimes, no doubt)
>   The good husband, as meek as a lamb,
>   Her vapours to still,
>   First grants her her will,
>   And the quieting draught is a dram;
>   Poor man! and the quieting draught is a dram.
>   I wish all our quarrels might have so comfortable a
>   reconciliation.
> POLLY: I have no excuse for my own behaviour, madam,
>   but my misfortunes—and really, madam, I suffer
>   too upon your account.

Polly's polite claim to altruism, whether or not it has a sincerity which would only be pathetic, acts as an insult, and the dram ("in the way of friendship") is immediately proposed. Lucy is leading up to the poison in the song, but her diplomacy is so stylised as to become a comment of the author's. The quieting draught is death; no other medicine will bring peace or comfort to so restless a fragment of divinity. It is also alcohol; peace can only be obtained from what gives further excitement, because simple peace is not attainable in the world. Gin alone, however, she has just pointed out, is often enough quieting in the fullest sense, and the poetic connection between death and intoxication gives a vague rich memory of the blood of the sacrament and the apocalyptic wine of the wrath of God.

Poor man. He is a martyr to the fair, so that his weaknesses are due to his modish greatness of spirit; when a man takes this tone about himself he means that he considers himself very successful with women, and pays them out. Lucy is boasting of the strength of the spleen as a weapon against him. Poor man, more generally, because of the fundamental human contradictions that are displayed; he is a beast of prey forced to be sociable. And "poor man, in the end he kills her, and is no doubt hanged"—for the force of *and*, prominent and repeated, is to make giving a quieting draught something quite different from, and later than, the attempt to "give her will"—it might be only drink she willed for, and the attempt to give it once for all was anyway hopeless. The comparison of the dramatic and condemned thing—murder by poison—to the dull and almost universal one—quieting by drink—is used to show that the dramatic incident is a symbol or analysis of something universal. Afterwards (the double-irony trick) this both refutes itself and insists on its point more suggestively (appears analysis not symbol) by making us feel that the dramatic thing is itself universal—the good meek husband, whether by poison or plain gin, is as much a murderer as Lucy. From whatever cause there is a queer note of triumph in the line.

The attempted murder is called a "comfort" chiefly because it is no more; to kill Polly won't get her back Macheath. And it fails because she finds Polly is not happy enough to deserve it; at the crucial moment Macheath is brought back in chains. There is no more need for murder in Lucy, because Macheath seems to have despised Polly's help, and anyway is separated from her. There is no more hope of "comfort" for Polly; she tosses gin and death together to the floor. So both women are left to poison his last moments. The playwright then refuses to kill Macheath, from the same cheerful piercing contempt; he is not dignified enough, he tells the audience, "though you think he is," to be made a tragic hero. Lucy's attempt is useless except for its ill-nature, which makes it seem a "typically human" and therefore pathetic piece of folly; she takes up an enthusiasm for murder because otherwise she would have to admit the facts (which the human creature can never afford to do) and give way to the "spleen" and despair—the spleen which is the despair of the most innocent and highly refined characters because to such characters this existence is essentially inadequate. Lucy's comic vanity in taking this tone (as in Macheath's different use of the device) is displayed only to be justified; "what better right has anyone else to it?"; it is not denied, such is the pathos of the effect, that the refined ladies may well take this tone, but they must not think it a specially exalted one. (To the Freudian, indeed, it is the human infant to whose desires this life is essentially inadequate; King Lear found a mystical pathos in the fact that the human infant, alone among the young of the creatures, is subject to impotent fits of fury.) It is this clash and identification of the refined, the universal, and the low that is the whole point of pastoral.

For the final meaning of this play, whose glory it is to give itself so wholeheartedly to vulgarisation, I can only list a few approaches to its irony. "I feel quite grateful to these fools; they make me feel sure I am right because they are so obviously wrong" (in this hopeful form satire is widely used to "keep people going" after loss of faith); "having got so far towards sympathy with the under-men, *non ragioniam di lor,* lest we come down to the *ultima ratio*" (Voltaire not talking politics to his valet); "one can see how impossible both the thieves and the politicians are if one compares them to heroes" (the polite literary assumption; the pose of detachment); "low as these men are, the old heroes were like them, and one may well feel the stronger for them; life was never dignified, and is still spirited." (The good spirits of Fielding making a Homeric parody of a village scuffle.) "The old heroes were much more like the modern thief than the modern aristocrat; the present order of society is based on an inversion of real values" (Pope sometimes made rather fussy local satire out of this); "this is always likely to happen; everything spiritual and valuable has a gross and revolting parody, very similar to it, with same name; only unremitting effort can distinguish between them" (Swift); "this always happens; no human distinction between high and low can be accepted for a moment; Christ on earth found no fit company but the thieves" (none of them accepted the full weight of the anarchy of this, but none of them forgot it; perhaps the mere easiness of Gay makes one feel it in him most easily). It is a fine thing that the play is still popular, however stupidly it is enjoyed.

Mercenary Fathers, Possessive Daughters, and Macheath

Martin Price

In *The Beggar's Opera* we find . . . a symmetrical disposition of characters. The play opens with a fine presentation of the inverted mercantile world of the Peachums. This world operates by the cash nexus alone, but it assumes its values with prim respectability. The tone of the play is extraordinarily complex, as William Empson has shown: the Peachums present an outrageously straight-faced asser- tion of thorough acquisitiveness with all the false unction of bour- geois stuffiness. So straight-faced is their parody of the conduct of their betters that they create a world highly formalized and "rhetor- ical." Their speeches, like all those in the play, suggest that no man can endure to think as little of himself as he deserves; all must con- sole themselves with some form of righteous cant. Their use of this cant is so handsomely stylized that it never quite seems the conven- tional self-deception men need in real life; instead, it has, as they perform, a delicious absurdity, with a constant undertone of bitter wit as one applies it to the actualities the play never directly admits.

This is, perhaps, a roundabout way of getting at a unique ef- fect. The play invites us at once to enjoy freedom from moral judg- ment and accept the comic ease of this world, where the "paradox of trade and morality" is so easily resolved into the values of trade and the gestures of morality. In this aspect, it is like those comic and pastoral works (it was undertaken, at Swift's urging, as a "Newgate pastoral") in which the conflicts of moral existence are

From *To the Palace of Wisdom: Studies in Order and Energy from Dryden to Blake.* © 1964 by Martin Price. Southern Illinois University Press, 1964.

banished. Yet, at every point, the play creates a satiric simplification of the conduct that governs the "high" world of Walpole and the court. Neither of these aspects—the comic and the satiric—can be ignored. The pastoral simplicity is not virtue opposed to a corrupt and complex court, but corruption reduced to artless ease, its humbug so effortless and thoroughgoing that it seems to criticize only the ineptitude of actual hypocrites. One may recall Pope's emphasis on the healthy freedom that dares "laugh out"; there is a relief in the comparative decency of frank assertion, even when it is presented by characters who pretend not to recognize its import. Gay's method can, I think, be traced back to such a work as Swift's *Argument against Abolishing Christianity,* where the projector offers the comfortable meaninglessness of "nominal Christianity" in opposition to a strenuous and unreliable effort to legislate Christianity out of existence. It is a method, as I have suggested [elsewhere], that [Bernard de] Mandeville used as well.

The Peachum household anticipates the family of Clarissa Harlowe in its righteous distrust of the aristocrat: he is not only dissolute, he is unpredictable, for he observes standards they cannot admit. Polly stands out as a creature who is spontaneous and unguarded. She has been seduced by a mock aristocrat who has lent her romances (the counterpart of Millamant's reading in the Cavalier poets); they have opened visions of a more generous life than her parents can conceive. Polly's last words in the first act catch very well a self-dramatizing rhetoric, an unconscious identifying of herself with the romance heroine: "O how I fear! how I tremble!— Go—but when safety will give you leave, you will be sure to see me again; for 'till then Polly is wretched." This note of the romantic and histrionic is present earlier, as Polly considers Macheath's possible end:

> Methinks I see him already in the cart, sweeter and more lovely than the nosegay in his hand!—I hear the crowd extolling his resolution and intrepidity!—What vollies of sighs are sent from the windows of Holborn, that so comely a youth should be brought to disgrace! I see him at the tree! The whole Circle are in tears!—even Butchers weep!
>
> (act 1, sc. 12)

There is a telling difference between this ardent mixture of alarm and erotic daydream and the crisp finality of Mrs. Peachum's

"Hang your husband, and be dutiful," or Peachum's sententious "The comfortable estate of widowhood, is the only hope that keeps up a wife's spirits." Polly's emotion is more generous; it comes closer to the full range of human feeling than any other in the play, and it is reduced to a degree of comic unreality by its literary quality, its air of being something newly learned and not wholly mastered, however sincerely spoken. Gay makes romantic love a kind of child's masquerade in this world, as opposed to the more knowing game the elders seem to be playing.

But Polly herself suffers as the symmetry of the play develops. The second act gives us the world of the outlaw. The Gang are men who risk their lives for what they get. They depend upon each other for their safety, and their dependence builds a loyalty beyond the appeal of interest. They are at once more careless and more generous than the elder Peachums, and they live by a code of honor to which they trust their survival. It is in their swaggering boast of their purpose that their spirit of freedom is best stated:

> We retrench the superfluities of mankind. The world is avaritious, and I hate avarice. A covetous fellow, like a Jack-daw, steals what he was never made to enjoy, for the sake of hiding it. These are the robbers of mankind, for money was made for the full-hearted and generous, and where is the injury of taking from another, what he hath not the heart to make use of?
>
> (act 2, sc. 1)

The opposition of avarice and generosity sets up the central contrast of the play and prepares us for Macheath's disclosure: "Polly is most confoundedly bit.—I love the sex. And a man who loves money might as well be contented with one guinea, as I with one woman" (2.3). Just as Polly is free of the grasping avarice of her parents, so Macheath is free of the possessive loyalty of her love. He is a natural aristocrat, a man of style: "I must have women. There is nothing unbends the mind like them." And his treatment of his doxies shows a fine sense of tone, a feeling for the manner of address each must have. Macheath is even more unguarded than Polly: he is incapable of any surrender of his freedom. He has no higher use for it than to enjoy it, certainly; but his love of the sex, like his captaincy of a gang of outlaws, makes his life the more precarious. If his love of women be the "flaw" in his mock-tragic character, the pursuit of freedom is perhaps its more serious basis, and, curiously, the quality that makes him more romantic than any of Polly's daydreams. Gay insists upon him as a somewhat shabby seducer and a tavern swell, but the "high" note Macheath somewhat fastidiously borrows from Shakespeare ("If musick be the food of Love, play on," from *Twelfth Night;* and paraphrasing *Antony and Cleopatra:* "Was this well done, Jenny?") alludes to a vanished nobility as surely as do the gestures of the playing cards in *The Rape of the Lock.*

Once the symmetry of Peachum and Lockit is established, Macheath's solitary career is set between paired characters as tenacious as manacles: the mercenary fathers and the possessive daughters. "If you had been kind to me 'till death," exclaims Polly, "it would not have vex'd me—And that's no very unreasonable request (though from a wife) to a man who hath not above seven or eight days to live" (2.13). The girls are simpler, far less assured and deft in their intrigues, but they are in some measure their fathers' daughters. Macheath, on the other hand, for all his operatic self-dramatization and self-pity, comes to a stark awareness that is all but tragic. "That that Jemmy Twitcher should peach me, I own surpriz'd me!—'Tis a plain proof that the world is all alike, and that even our Gang can no more trust one another than other people. Therefore, I beg you, gentlemen, look well to yourselves, for in all probability you may live some months longer" (3.14). It is too much to say that he comes to accept his own nature as part of this world's, but the firm understatement would serve such a meaning in another kind of play.

Gay's lovers, then, seem to divide, Polly into the way of organized society, with its legal bonds and imprisoning institutions, Macheath into the way of outlawry, freedom from involvement, and therefore utter vulnerability. As Lockit puts it, "Of all animals of prey, man is the only sociable one. Every one of us preys upon his neighbours, and yet we herd together." But the play cannot end so, and the Beggar imposes upon it an ending such as the taste of the town requires. The Beggar's manipulation is, in one sense, a symbolic selling out in key with the world he has presented.

But even before this last insistence upon artifice is made, Gay has overturned Macheath's moment of tragic eloquence with the introduction of four more wives, "with a child a-piece." Macheath dwindles from a noble solitary to a master of ineptitude, and the way is clear for a return to sentiment: "I take Polly for mine.—And for life, you Slut,—for we were really marry'd." We are back in the world of comedy, where the exceptional hero is as much fool as prophet, and where Polly's bungling goodness of heart finds its appropriate reward. The lovers are lovers, after all, and Macheath's seeming superiority to the captivity of marriage has been part of the somewhat tawdry swagger of a role too big to sustain. Polly, who has neither her parents' art nor Macheath's grandeur, has captured this world for bourgeois romance. What gives the play part at least of its peculiar force is Gay's willingness to explore conflicting views to the uttermost; they must be resolved by contrivance, finally, but the contrivance seems, after all, the inevitable. Macheath is not "lost above" this world; but he has been allowed to enjoy the histrionic illusion for a while. And Polly is not simply the helpless victim of a savage world; she has the tenacity of her parents without their coldness. These characters never begin to know themselves, nor do they control their fate; but Gay, like Fielding later, plays the just god in his creation.

The Beggar's Triumph

Patricia Meyer Spacks

It is, of course, for *The Beggar's Opera* that Gay is remembered in
the twentieth century, even among people with no particular interest in eighteenth-century poetry or drama. The play was revived in
a rather romanticized London production with great success in
1926; its music was later adapted and presented by Benjamin Britten; in 1963 the Royal Shakespeare Company produced it once
more, with great attention to realistic detail, and with a vivid sense
of the play's topicality in modern England, once more riddled with
scandal in high places. Made into a movie starring Laurence Oliv-
ier, *The Beggar's Opera* still returns to art theaters; it has been reis-
sued in formats ranging from an inexpensive student paperback to a
splendid reproduction of the 1729 edition; a new recording recently
presented all its music and much of its speech.

Probably nothing, however, has brought Gay's work so much
to popular attention as the fact that *The Beggar's Opera* was the basis
for Bertolt Brecht's *Threepenny Opera,* which relied on it for broad
plot structure, for many of its characters, and even for some of its
music. The Brecht play, which had a record-breaking run off-
Broadway, seems lively and singularly relevant; it has led some
readers to new awareness of comparable qualities in Gay's opera,
which conveys so highly sophisticated a structure of qualifications
that its subject almost seems to be the nature and necessity of qualification in life. In its awareness of the immense difficulty of civi-
lized existence, it speaks directly to our own time.

From *John Gay.* © 1965 by Twayne Publishers, Inc.

The relevance of *The Beggar's Opera* to the twentieth century was underlined by its most recent London production, a Brechtian version in which slight textual alterations stressed the applicability of Gay's satire to such modern phenomena as the Profumo affair (e.g., "I, Madam, was once kept by a Tory."). In a "preview" published in the *Manchester Guardian* the day before the play's London opening, Philip Hope-Wallace speculated about the modern effect of the comedy. "Will anyone be shocked now?" he asks, and concludes that it is "a question of age perhaps." "I should think," adds Hope-Wallace, "this indestructible old bag of other men's tunes and its comedy within a comedy would be exactly to modern taste and once again become the talk of the town."

He was, however, rather too optimistic. Although the play's audiences were clearly amused and refreshed by the satiric energy of the "opera" in Peter Wood's production, which employed an elaborate and ingenious set, stylized action, broad parody, and deliberate techniques of "alienation," the newspaper critics were less enthusiastic. They revived the issues of the eighteenth century: the *Sunday Times* commentator, alone in liking the play, praised Polly, like his predecessors two hundred years before, as "an unquenchable sunbeam in a world of tumultuous shadows." Other critics returned to the question of morality. "Morality does not suit an eighteenth-century comedy," wrote David Pryce-Jones [in *The Spectator*], "particularly one so sensitive as *The Beggar's Opera,* where all the lessons to be learnt are implied and all the criticism is self-contained." Kenneth Tynan had similar objections: "What should be implied is shrieked aloud (*The Observer*)." The problem remains: how can moral satire be made clear and convincing without becoming too blatant? Gay solved that problem largely through his conception of the play; the modern producer, by trying to stress through setting (the play takes place on a prison ship), realistic costume, and stylized action the indictment of social conditions implicit in *The Beggar's Opera,* apparently made that indictment less palatable.

In considering the *Fables* [elsewhere] we discovered that the nature of their form helped Gay to achieve success. The same is true of *The Beggar's Opera:* the special variety of dramatic form that Gay here chose was maximally useful in solving the problems that plagued him. He had long experimented with various uses of disguise in drama; now he developed a form almost completely dependent on disguise. He could actually introduce himself directly into his play, given the disguise (and a very significant one it is, considering his preoccupation with money) of beggar.

The importance of this mask as a distancing device becomes apparent when we compare the Introduction of *The Beggar's Opera* with that of its sequel, *Polly*. The first words of the Beggar in the earlier play are these: "If Poverty be a Title to Poetry, I am sure Nobody can dispute mine. I own my self of the Company of Beggars; and I make one at their Weekly Festivals at St. *Gile's*. I have a small Yearly Salary for my Catches, and am welcome to a Dinner there whenever I please, which is more than most Poets can say." The charm of this speech comes chiefly from the fact that the poet thinks of himself *mainly* as beggar, only secondarily as poet; from this perspective he can treat the financial need characteristic of poets with saving irony. He does not appear to take himself or his poetry very seriously; extolling the pleasures of beggarhood, he thus makes a telling comment on the difficulties of being a poet (his point, of course, is that the beggar is *more* independent than the typical poet). But he manages to avoid pathos and distasteful self-concern: his self-esteem is, for a change, appealing rather than unattractive.

His counterpart in *Polly*, on the other hand, is called not *beggar* but *poet*. The disguise is much thinner, and the language of the character reflects his greater closeness to the actual nature of the author: "A Sequel to a play is like more last words. It is a kind of absurdity; and really, sir, you have prevailed upon me to pursue this subject against my judgment. . . . I know, I must have been looked upon as whimsical, and particular, if I had scrupled to have risqued my reputation for my profit; for why should I be more squeamish than my betters? and so, sir, contrary to my opinion, I bring *Polly* once again upon the stage." This is Gay speaking virtually in his own voice. After the wit of the first sentence, the speech degenerates into a sort of apology which upon analysis becomes increasingly distasteful. The point seems to be that the author *is*, in fact, offering this play for the sake of personal profit, but that his mode of admitting this is intended to remove our onus from him. He retains the rather unpleasant tone of moral superiority with no evidence of any real claim to such elevation. One important effect of the series of disguises in *The Beggar's Opera* is to make all pretensions to superiority into jokes; nothing in *Polly* reveals the Poet's claim as ludicrous. But the joke is necessary; the perspective it provides is a major—perhaps *the* major—source of strength in *The Beggar's Opera*.

Of course the disguise of Beggar for the author is only the first of many masks in *The Beggar's Opera;* all serve similar purposes of implicit commentary. The other disguises in the play are more complicated and less obvious than the introductory one, and they are difficult to define. Is one to say, for example, that Macheath is essentially an aristocrat in the disguise of a highwayman? Or is it more accurate to say that the highwayman in the play disguise themselves to themselves as aristocrats? Here is a sample of dialogue among Macheath's gang:

> NED: Who is there here that would not dye for his
> Friend?
> HARRY: Who is there here that would betray him for his
> Interest?
> MATT: Show me a Gang of Courtiers that can say as
> much.
> BEN: We are for a just Partition of the World, for every
> Man hath a Right to enjoy Life.
> MATT: We retrench the Superfluities of Mankind. The
> World is avaritious, and I hate Avarice. A covetous
> fellow, like a Jack-daw, steals what he was never
> made to enjoy, for the sake of hiding it. These are
> the Robbers of Mankind, for Money was made for
> the Free-hearted and Generous, and where is the
> Injury of taking from another, what he hath not the
> Heart to make use of?

These are aristocrats indeed: honorable, loyal, governed by principle; and if the principles seem to partake largely of rationalization, surely this fact makes the gang seem no less *aristocratic*. We get a different, but equally convincing, view of the highwayman as aristocrat from the Peachums, who, as William Empson has demonstrated, represent the bourgeois perspective in the play.

> MRS. PEACHUM: I knew she was always a proud Slut; and
> now the wench hath play'd the Fool and married,
> because forsooth she would do like the Gentry. Can
> you support the Expense of a Husband, Hussy, in
> gaming, drinking and whoring? . . . If you must be

> married, could you introduce no-body into our
> Family but a Highwayman? Why, thou foolish Jade,
> thou wilt be as ill-us'd, and as much neglected, as if
> thou hadst married a Lord!
>
> PEACHUM: Let not your Anger, my Dear, break through
> the Rules of Decency, for the Captain looks upon
> himself in the Military Capacity, as a Gentleman by
> his Profession.

Earlier, before the marriage is revealed, the Peachums discuss Macheath's wealth and prospects. They agree that he keeps good company and associates with the gentry, but this tendency is a weakness: he cannot expect to win at the gaming tables without the education of a fine gentleman. "What business hath he to keep Company with Lords and Gentlemen?" Mrs. Peachum concludes: "he should leave them to prey upon one another." To be aristocrats means, then, in this world, *not* to be men of honor and principle, but to be men who prey on one another.

William Hazlitt, assuming the identity between aristocrat and gentleman, finds Macheath heroic indeed:

> Macheath should be a fine man and a gentleman, but he
> should be one of God Almighty's gentlemen, not a gen-
> tleman of the black rod. His gallantry and good-breeding
> should arise from impulse, not from rule; not from the
> trammels of education, but from a soul generous, coura-
> geous, good-natured, aspiring, amorous. The class of the
> character is very difficult to hit. It is something between
> gusto and slang, like port-wine and brandy mixed. It is
> not the mere gentleman that should be represented, but
> the blackguard sublimated into the gentleman. This char-
> acter is qualified in a highwayman, as it is qualified in a
> prince. We hope this is not a libel.

This image of Macheath as nature's nobleman is appealing, but the play will not allow us to rest content with it. Just at the point where we may be tempted to say that the highwaymen are true aristocrats, the nobility false ones, we discover that Macheath, for example, despite his prating of honor, is as capable of treachery, as proud of his seductions and their ultimate effect in populating Drury Lane (the resort of prostitutes) as his "betters" could conceivably be.

Similarly, our vision of Polly is made to fluctuate wildly. Eighteenth-century audiences wept and applauded at Polly's song, "Oh ponder well! be not severe," responding to its pathos and to her as a pathetic heroine. She has, to be sure, all the postures of the traditional romantic lead: her frequent evocations of the idea of love, her parroting of the notions of playbooks (although, to be sure, her admission of their source rather tempers the potency of such notions), her quite unjustified faith in Macheath's loyalty and her unwillingness to betray him—all these characteristics are conventionally admirable. But the first words of this Polly, who insists on her sentimentality and her virtue, spoken to her father, are, "I know as well as any of the fine Ladies how to make the most of my self and my Man too. A Woman knows how to be mercenary, though she hath never been in a Court or at an Assembly. We have it in our Natures, Papa."

This is not, to be sure, a direct statement of Polly's own feelings: she wishes at the moment to obscure her actual marriage to Macheath by pretending to conform precisely to her father's standards. But she has the lesson a bit too pat for comfort: it is easy to suspect that she really partakes of these values. After all, the truth is that she *does,* as she claims, have such visible marks of the captain's favor as a watch. The song she sings immediately after this speech ("Virgins are like the fair Flower in its Lustre") emphasizes the commodity view of virginity; when, later in the play, Polly comes into contact with Lucy, who has loved not wisely but too well, her sense of superiority rests on the fact that she has been smart enough to make a better bargain than Lucy: marriage for virginity. William Empson documents her feverish interest in hanging, the extent to which she seems almost to desire what she most fears, Macheath's death by hanging, the only form which death takes in this play.

All this is not to say that Polly lacks charm; she is, of course, the play's most appealing character. But it is the nature of this play that its most charming personages are frequently undercut, while its least attractive figures have moments of such moral clarity that we can hardly reject them. Thus the senior Peachums, underhanded, self-seeking, treacherous as they are, can convince us momentarily that the evils they abundantly demonstrate are merely natural concomitants of good business practice: they have the airs, the language, the self-esteem of successful businessmen; and our moral detestation of them cannot be quite secure—particularly if we perceive their resemblance to modern representatives of the business world. All the characters of *The Beggar's Opera* could be transferred to a new plot about the participants in a television quiz show scandal with little change in their natures or their comments. The play leaves us with no secure stance; in place of one perspective from which to view the characters, it offers many. These characters do not come on stage in the casing of a mummy or a crocodile. They are disguised even *from themselves;* they do not know what they really are. As a consequence it becomes difficult for us to know what they are. This is a far more subtle use of the disguise motif than Gay ever made before or later; it dramatizes the almost metaphysical implications of the device.

II

If the shifting self-disguises (Polly as her father's daughter, as sentimental heroine, as wronged wife; Macheath as honorable gentleman, as dishonorable seducer; the Peachums as practical business people, as despicable profiteers in vice) afford one mode of constant qualification in the play, another is provided by the patterns of imagery which run through songs and prose alike. William Empson has discussed brilliantly and in some detail the imagery of hanging and its ramifications. Two other themes of the imagery are almost equally obvious: money and animals. And the three patterns in conjunction provide interesting commentary on one another.

The image of human beings as animals, a favorite of Gay's, becomes in *The Beggar's Opera* a subtle and complicated device. Lockit's direct summary of the motif is well-known: "Lions, Wolves, and Vulturs don't live together in Herds, Droves or Flocks.—Of all Animals of Prey, Man is the only sociable one. Every one of us preys upon his Neighbour, and yet we herd together.—*Peachum* is my Companion, my Friend—According to the Custom of the World, indeed, he may quote thousands of Precedents for cheating me—And shall I not make use of the Privilege of Friendship to make him a Return?" In tone and emphasis this speech is wonderfully characteristic of the play. It parodies the note of self-satisfaction we hear so often in these characters: Lockit is smug over the "superiority" of man, demonstrated by his sociability, to other vicious animals with an immediate exposition of precisely what this sociability means in practice. But the play provides many more specific statements of the similarity between men and animals.

It seems—although there are many exceptions—that the women in the play are somewhat more likely to think of love in animal terms, while the men connect love directly with money. Mrs. Peachum sees the "simple Maid" as a moth, constantly playing about the flame until, if she is not made a wife, her honor's singed ("If Love the Virgin's Heart invade"). Polly describes the virgin as a flower, with her lovers as bees and butterflies ("Virgins are like the fair Flower in its Lustre"). Later, in a sentimental song, she likens herself to a turtledove ("The Turtle thus with plaintive crying"). Again, immediately after Macheath, masculine and money-oriented, has compared his love for her to that of a miser for his shilling, she compares hers for him to that of a boy for his sparrow ("The Miser thus a Shilling sees"). Jenny Diver, one of the trulls, sees Macheath as a cock attended by hens ("Before the Barn-door crowing").

All these images, with the possible exception of Polly's boy-sparrow one, are comparatively innocent, although in the total context of the play they seem less so than we might expect. Gradually, though, the connections between human love and the animal world become increasingly sinister. Macheath, betrayed by women, shifts the bird imagery to a new realm: "Women are Decoy Ducks; who can trust them! Beasts, Jades, Jilts, Harpies, Furies, Whores!" When Lucy confronts her betrayer, Macheath, in prison, she sings a song which makes him the trapped rat and her the good housewife who throws it to the dog or cat ("Thus when a good Huswife sees a Rat"). Polly, still dwelling on bird imagery, compares herself to a female, Macheath to a male swallow, in a song whose point, Empson suggests, is that she is eagerly awaiting Macheath's death ("Thus when the Swallow, seeking Prey"). Then Lucy sees herself as a fox, Macheath as another ("I like the Fox shall grieve"). The final two songs in this sequence of animal lyrics are worth quoting in full. The first is sung by Lockit to Peachum, as he suggests that Macheath can be trapped by keeping an eye on Polly:

> What Gudgeons are we Men!
> Ev'ry Woman's easy Prey.
> Though we have felt the Hook, agen
> We bite and they betray.

> The Bird that hath been trapt,
> When he hears his calling Mate,
> To her he flies, again he's clapt
> Within the wiry Grate.

The second is sung alternately by Polly and Lucy:

> POLLY: A Curse attends that Woman's
> Love. Who always would be
> pleasing.
> LUCY: The Pertness of the billing Dove,
> Like tickling, is but teazing.
> POLLY: What then in Love can Woman do?
> LUCY: If we grow fond they shun us.
> POLLY: And when we fly them, they
> pursue:
> LUCY: But leave us when they've won us.

The songs comment tellingly on the sentimentality of some of the previous uses of bird imagery. Lockit's lyrics are particularly explicit, juxtaposing the image of men as "poor fish" to be hooked by women with an even more sinister picture of female birds as decoys to trap the males. All attempts to glamorize the notion of human beings as animals or birds must ultimately fail; this is degrading imagery, and Lockit, for the moment at least, sees it quite explicitly as such. (It is also Lockit, incidentally, who provides the most menacing animal image of the play: "Like Pikes, lank with Hunger, who miss of their Ends, / They bite their Companions, and prey on their Friends.") Polly and Lucy, from the opposite, feminine, point of view, perceive the same truth: they may try to romanticize their roles, but the actuality is hard and inescapable.

The pattern of animal imagery, in other words, provides its own commentary. Moving in general from benign to vicious images, it also moves from the unself-conscious, romantic, and conventional to a more cynical and analytical use of the same sort of material. And the later usages reflect back on the earlier ones, causing us to feel that innocence in this world (whatever innocence Polly truly had at first) can be equated only with ignorance, that romanticism is a resource only for those who know nothing of reality.

The notion of human beings as animals is further illuminated by frequent metaphorical and literal remarks about money. Love and money are, of course, closely related: Filch's first song establishes the nature of the relationship:

> 'Tis Woman that seduces all Mankind,
> By her we first were taught the wheedling Arts:
> Her very eyes can cheat; when most she's kind,
> She tricks us of our Money with our Hearts.
> For her, like Wolves by night we roam for Prey,
> And practise ev'ry Fraud to bribe her Charms;
> For Suits of Love, like Law, are won by Pay,
> And Beauty must be fee'd into our Arms.

This song not only summarizes the masculine point of view toward "love," as it exists in the world of the play; it also suggests the relation between human emphasis on money and the notion of human beings as animals. Men become wolves, Filch says quite explicitly, because of the feminine demand for money. And since, as other songs and comments in the play make abundantly clear, virtually *every* human enterprise depends upon money, it is quite apparent that man can hardly escape reduction to animality.

Mrs. Peachum is the only woman in the play who states explicitly that women themselves are commodities of equivalent value to money. She sees the maid as "like the golden Oar, / Which hath Guineas intrinsical in't"; the precise value of the ore is unknown until it is minted. The wife, on the other hand, is "like a Guinea in Gold, / Stampt with the Name of her Spouse"; although she no longer has the advantage of being of incalculable value, she acquires a new benefit: that of being an accepted medium of exchange, "current in every House." "The first time a Woman is frail, she should be somewhat nice methinks, for then or never is the time to make her fortune." This is Mrs. Peachum's morality, and, if no other woman quite states it, there is little evidence that anyone has an essentially different standard. Polly sees Macheath as her "treasure"; she also seems to have had a good sense of the value of her virginity, though she would not use such crass terms as her mother.

"You might sooner tear a Pension out of the Hands of a Courtier, a Fee from a Lawyer, a pretty Woman from a Looking-glass, or any Woman from Quadrille.—But to tear me from thee is impossible!" This is Macheath's idea of a fitting protestation of love to Polly, who, in the play's comedy, accepts it quite blandly as such. More consistently than anyone else, he connects love with money. His metaphor of Polly as the shilling, himself as the miser, seems surprising: more often he values women in terms of guineas: "A Man who loves Money, might as well be contented with one Guinea, as I with one Woman." And again, "I must have Women. There is nothing unbends the Mind like them. Money is not so strong a Cordial for the Time."

Hazlitt may include Macheath's "amorousness" among his virtues, but this particular aspect of the captain's high regard for women is hardly attractive. The trulls he has sent to Drury Lane share his values: one praises another because, "Though her Fellow be never so agreeable, she can pick his Pocket as cooly, as if Money were her only Pleasure. Now that is a Command of the Passions uncommon in a Woman!" After one of them betrays the captain (for money), they argue over their "accounts": how many hanged men should be laid to the credit of each. Macheath himself is greeted in prison by Lucy, whom he has seduced and left pregnant; one of her songs to him ends:

> Whoever steals a Shilling,
> Through Shame the Guilt conceals:
> In Love the perjur'd Villain
> With Boasts the Theft reveals.

And there is justice in her complaint. Macheath convinces her that he plans to marry her, but she is unable to soften her father's heart. Macheath suggests that in such a case a bribe is indicated: "Money well tim'd, and properly apply'd, will do any thing." His next song elaborates the point, concluding that the way to win a woman is to offer her money: "That Reason with all is prevailing." "In the Account of Love you are in my debt," Macheath tells Lucy. "Owe thy Life to me," Lucy replies. But as Macheath points out a bit later, "Death is a Debt, / A Debt on demand"—and a gentleman always pays debts of this sort, if not those of love.

Of course these examples in the play do not even begin to exhaust the discussion of money, its function and its effects. But the ways in which money is connected with love—or with what passes for love in the play—are particularly indicative of the total corruption of the world described here. Filch makes a living by "helping the Ladies to a Pregnancy against their being called down to Sentence"—by eighteenth-century law pregnant women could not be hanged. Sven Armens comments accurately on this fact:

Here sexual intercourse, which can be the warm expression of true love, has been most thoroughly debased. Even lust itself has been undermined. Love is moral and practical; lust is immoral and impractical; but begetting illegitimate children in order to cheat justice combines immorality with a sort of practicality. This is sex as simply business for all concerned; a breed farm for criminals represents the complete perversion of the chivalric code of courtly love.

Except for Polly, sex seems to be hardly more than business for anyone in the play; even Lucy, who claims to be desperately in love, is capable of bargaining over her sexual rights. The Peachums consider their daughter a business asset; Polly herself can deal with her virginity as a commodity; Macheath makes little distinction between the pursuits of love and of money; Lockit thinks of love and money as equivalent material for bargaining. The money-love imagery sums up and emphasizes the nature of a society completely dominated by money—for frequent references in the play insist that lawyers, courtiers, doctors—all the world—care only for money; and Lockit and Peachum, those companions in crime, fall out before our eyes over their profits.

"Money well tim'd, and properly apply'd, will do any thing." "Of all Animals of Prey, Man is the only sociable one." Considered in conjunction, these two thematic statements explain and reflect upon one another. The cause of man's preying and of his sociability, as expounded in this play, is money. Or, conversely, the reason that money will do anything is that man is an animal of prey. His prey is only incidentally other human beings, ultimately it is money. Fierce punitive measures dispose of the weak, the poor, the unlucky in such a society: this brings us to the matter of hanging, the source of the third major pattern of imagery. Love, death, and money; human beings reducing themselves to a subanimal level—it sounds a somber play indeed. And of course it *is* somber—but funny as well; for the involved structure of cross-commentary, keeping the reader constantly a little off-balance, forces him to see the ridiculous as well as the horrible aspects of each situation.

The ending of the play is a perfect instance of the way in which this particular double view (of the world as both horrifying and ridiculous) is maintained. Macheath is about to be hanged when the player of the introduction protests to the beggar-author that an opera must end happily. The beggar agrees to cry a reprieve for Macheath; the player approves: "All this we must do, to comply with the Taste of the Town." Sven Armens summarizes the implications of this piece of action by observing, "The moral of the play is dismissed as the town in its ethical degradation dismisses morality." True enough—here is the horror: that the "town" which witnesses the play is a society of the same sort as that depicted in the play equally corrupt, equally perverted in values, and that honest drama, which shows "that the lower Sort of People have their Vices in a degree as well as the Rich: and that they are punish'd for them," is consequently impossible. But it is equally true (and of course Sven Armens elsewhere demonstrates his awareness of the play's comic aspects) that the superb inconsequence of the ending accords tonally with the general lightheartedness of the play as a whole, lightheartedness which persists, paradoxically, despite the bitterness, the intense cynicism reiterated by the ending. It is quite proper to laugh at these matters—if one can retain the perspective of an outsider and fail to realize that he also is being condemned. And it is proper also to abhor and denounce the world depicted: the one response is incomplete without the other.

III

An obvious aspect of *The Beggar's Opera* which we will in the main have to ignore is its music. Most operas, even comic operas, hardly exist for the average reader outside their stage productions; their music supplies justification or compensation for the improbabilities of their plots, their eccentricities of language and meter. It is a measure of how remarkable Gay's accomplishment was that his play has such vivid life even on the printed page, its songs self-justified by the charm of their lyrics. But the music of *The Beggar's Opera* adds an extra dimension to the play on stage—and Gay used this resource, too, in his elaborate structure of cross-commentary.

The commentary comes from the relation of Gay's lyrics to the original words attached to the music. Almost all the songs in the play are traditional tunes (hence the name of the genre created by this work: *ballad opera*), and the lyrics originally connected with them would have been familiar to the early audiences. A recent edition of the play has printed texts of the early songs side by side with Gay's versions, and some comparisons are instructive. Many have been pointed out by Professor Bronson in the essay [elsewhere] cited. In general, they intensify the same implications we have discovered already. When Mrs. Peachum sings of how maids are like gold ore, wives like gold guineas, she sings to a tune which earlier had words insisting that:

> We're just like a Mouse in a Trap,
> Or Vermin caught in a Gin;
> We Sweat and Fret, and try to Escape
> And Curse the sad Hour we came in.

Thus the imagery of money is in effect placed in conjunction with that of animals—the precise metaphor of the mouse in a trap is to be used later by Lucy. The song, " 'Tis Woman that seduces all Mankind" goes with a tune whose words describe a masculine seducer who loves and leaves his victims: if listeners are conscious of the traditional version, they are by this very fact prevented from having a simple view of the situation. Macheath's sentimental song, "Pretty Polly, say," is based on a piece beginning "Pretty Parret say"—and this in itself is adequate comment on the captain's sentimentality. (Indeed, the view of Polly as parrot sheds light on her apparent complexity: her ideas are secondhand, derived from diverse sources; she recites whatever seems appropriate in a specific situation.) The lyric beginning, "No power on earth can e'er divide / The knot that sacred Love hath ty'd" must be considered in conjunction with its predecessor:

> Remember Damon you did tell,
> In Chastity you lov'd me well,
> But now alas I am undone,
> And here am left to make my Moan.

So much for professions of everlasting and sacred love!

These sketchy examples should be enough to emphasize once more the consistency with which Gay insisted upon keeping his readers and audiences simultaneously conscious of different—often radically different—perspectives on the action, the characters, the very language of his play. The Beggar's Opera is a work of enormous sophistication, unprecedented in Gay's literary career and never again to be equaled or even approached by him. When he attempted immediately to duplicate his success by reusing the same characters in Polly, the result was a literary—although by no means a financial—fiasco. And perhaps the best way to conclude a discussion of *The Beggar's Opera* is by a brief examination of its sequel, which demonstrates by its failure to employ them how valuable the devices of the earlier play are.

IV

The early history of *Polly* is more interesting than the play itself. The comedy was finished late in 1728. Although it was far more innocent politically than *The Beggar's Opera,* in December its performance was prohibited on vague political grounds by the lord chamberlain. (As Gay himself put it, "I am accused, in general terms, of having written many disaffected libels and seditious pamphlets.") W. E. Schultz suggests the probability that the prohibition depended not so much on the content of the play as on the fact "that the report of a new play bearing Gay's name was . . . unfit for the comfort of the Walpole circle." At any rate, the play could be printed if not acted, with the prospect of the added sales that censorship always seems to bring. Within a year 10,500 copies had been sold of two large quarto editions. Estimates of Gay's actual proceeds vary wildly: Schultz believes that the playwright may have made £3,000; James Sutherland suggests £1,000. At any rate, immediate pirated editions reduced his receipts: the first piracies appeared within three or four days after the original publication of *Polly,* early in April 1729, and by June there were injunctions for piracy against seventeen printers and booksellers. Evidently a good many others felt, with Gay, that a sequel to *The Beggar's Opera* could hardly fail.

But, whatever its receipts, the play remains a failure. *The Beggar's Opera* presents us with a world in which *everyone* is corrupt: we may discern differences of degree, but no real distinctions of kind. Filch, the youth who makes his living by causing pregnancies, has his moments of charm; Polly, that delightful heroine, has hers of unpleasant calculation. In *Polly,* on the other hand, society splits into heroes and villains; there is no doubt at all where one's sympathies are to lie. Polly has become a model of virtue; we are expected to take with entire seriousness her protestations of undying love to Macheath, although at the end of the play, having discovered Macheath's full villainy, she appears ready to marry a noble savage who is also, conveniently, a prince.

Her speech at this juncture is characteristic of her language throughout: "I am charm'd, prince, with your generosity and virtue. 'Tis only by the pursuit of those we secure real happiness. Those that know and feel virtue in themselves, must love it in others. Allow me to give a decent time to my sorrows. But my misfortunes at present interrupt the joys of victory." It is almost inconceivable that Gay could offer us such speech with no ironic perspective, but here and throughout the play he does exactly that. The Indians are without exception noble, so their language must be noble, too; the pirates, invariably villainous, talk always like villains.

Macheath has now painted himself black (a convenient symbol), named himself *Morano,* and taken up with Jenny Diver, who managed to be transported with him. He is no longer the model of the highwayman-gentleman, having been morally destroyed by his unworthy love. When at the end he is finally hanged, we could hardly wish for a reprieve (indeed, one is actually granted, but too late): he has become so conventionally detestable that we find him both boring and distasteful and feel well rid of him. ("If justice hath overtaken him," says the Indian prince to Polly, with superb lack of logic, "he was unworthy of you.") The only interesting villain in the play is a minor one, Ducat, the plantation owner who originally buys Polly to be his concubine and who at the very last hopes still to make a profit from her. In Gay's depiction of him alone (and occasionally of Mrs. Trapes, a transplant from *The Beggar's Opera*), we find touches of the poet's old satiric insight.

It is significant that these minor figures should be the most successful characters in the play, for they are also the two who have the closest relation to eighteenth-century actuality. Ducat is struggling to follow the model of the English gentleman; Mrs. Trapes, his tutor, guides him in his progress in vice. Given this much relation to real society, these characters seem more meaningful than their companions; the Indians, the pirates, Macheath himself, certainly Polly, do not have much to do with reality, although the playwright frequently insists that Macheath and his band are allegorical representatives of the viciousness inherent in English society. In *The Beggar's Opera,* on the other hand, although the atmosphere is permeated with a delicious sense of unreality (we don't believe for a moment that highwaymen or "fences" ever talked like that; we don't believe in the action; the sudden shift at the ending is a surprise but not a shock, considering that none of the action has caused the suspension of disbelief), the total effect depends fundamentally on our constant, steady conviction that everything that happens on stage has its direct analogue on higher levels of society. Lacking the power to convey this conviction, *Polly* can only seem an essentially frivolous and meaningless exercise.

There's no use flogging a dead horse, and *Polly* is a very dead one indeed. Yet it provides a dramatic illustration of how precarious was the balance Gay established in *The Beggar's Opera*. Lacking that balance all other devices must fail. The imagery in *Polly* comes from the same realms as that of its predecessor; the songs are based on similar originals. But nothing works in *Polly,* and certainly no two devices work together. The difference between hackwork and comic drama informed by a vision can seldom have been so clearly demonstrated as in the relation between *The Beggar's Opera* and its sequel.

Mock-heroic Irony and the Comedy of Manners

Ronald Paulson

John Gay's *Beggar's Opera* was Fielding's most important source for the use of the heroic level as a parallel instead of a contrast to his subject. The diction and mock-heroic similes put into the mouths of Gay's robbers and whores do not allude to an ideal but rather show a correspondence between the activities of robbers and the heroic (or upper-class) activities their words evoke. The Beggar who acts as chorus makes the analogy between high and low explicit at the end of the performance:

> Through the whole piece you may observe such a similitude of manners in high and low Life, that it is difficult to determine whether (in the fashionable vices) the fine gentlemen imitate the gentlemen of the road, or the gentlemen of the road the fine gentlemen.—Had the Play remain'd, as I at first intended [i.e., with the robbers hanged and transported], it would have carried a most excellent moral. 'Twould have shown that the lower sort of people have their vices in a degree as well as the rich: And that they are punish'd for them.
>
> (act 3, sc. 16)

Gay's robbers, pimps, and whores sound and act like the much-admired heroes of Italian opera and speak in similes that relate their actions to those of lawyers, merchants, courtiers, and politicians.

From *Satire and the Novel in Eighteenth Century England.* © 1967 by Yale University. Yale University Press, 1967.

The inference is that opera heroes and politicians, underneath their rhetoric and respectability, have the same cutthroat values as Macheath and Peachum, the highwayman and the fence, but only the latter "are punish'd for them." Besides the upward thrust of the low-high analogy, there is an equally deadly thrust outward from the actors on the stage, whatever their roles, to the merchants and gentlemen in the audience. The implication of the Beggar's substitution of a happy ending for the hanging of Macheath is that the latter would have made all the Macheaths in the audience too uncomfortable.

Gay's low-high analogy is an ingenious satiric device, but of paramount importance to Fielding is the attempt to embody the mock-heroic relationship in a variety of character types, turning it into an inappropriate diction that reveals a character's upward aspiration—his desire to emulate the more respectable citizen and/or his hypocrisy—his middle-class desire to avoid calling a spade a spade. Each group in *The Beggar's Opera* has its own mock-heroic equivalent, its own diction, and its own set of glancing similes. The Peachums and Lockits—the fences and jailers—talk like merchants. For example, when Lockit puts Macheath in leg-irons, he is a merchant trying to sell apparel to a gentleman.

> Do but examine them, sir,—never was better work. How genteely they are made! They will fit as easy as a glove, and the nicest man in England might not be ashamed to wear them. *(He puts on the chains.)* If I had the best gentleman in the land in my custody, I could not equip him more handsomely.
>
> (act 1, sc. 7)

Both are very much aware of class distinctions. Macheath talks like a gentleman, with occasional lines from Shakespeare thrown in, and his diction is supported by the mock-heroic similes of the other characters. As Mrs. Peachum says of him, "Sure there is not a finer gentleman upon the road than the captain!" (1.4), adding that if Polly marries him she will be "as ill used, and as much neglected, as if thou hadst married a lord" (1.8).

The highwaymen's whores talk in the manner of ladies of fashion. "Pray, madam, were you ever in keeping?" asks Dolly Trull. "I hope, madam," replies Suky Tawdry, "I han't been so long upon the town but I have met with some good fortune as well as my neighbors." "Pardon me, madam, I meant no harm by the question; 'Twas only in the way of conversation," says Trull (2.5). In the same way, Polly Peachum and Lucy Lockit are essentially imitators of the heroines of romance or tragedy (Macheath has seduced Polly by giving her romances to read):

LUCY: *(speaking of Macheath)* Perfidious wretch!
POLLY: Barbarous husband!
LUCY: Hadst thou been hanged five months ago, I had been happy. . . . Flesh and blood can't bear my usage.
POLLY: Shall I not claim my own? Justice bids me speak.

(act 2, sc. 13)

While, as Mrs. Peachum notes, Polly "loves to imitate the fine ladies" (1.4), her version of gentility is out of heroic plays and Italian operas and represents another variation in the play of parody styles.

The Beggar's Opera shows what can happen when mock-heroic irony is applied with some consistency to a character: the final effect is not so much to direct the satire to the thieves' betters as to dramatize social classes on the move upward and thus produce a comedy of manners. We observe the highwayman who sees himself as an aristocrat, flaunting his gentility and generosity, and the thief-takers and jailers who see themselves as merchants, with ledgers always at hand and talk of respectability and duty on their lips. The middle-class values of the Peachums and Lockits, based entirely on the profit motive, are contrasted with the disinterested love of Polly and Lucy. Lucy, for example, tells her father: "One can't help love; one can't cure it. 'Tis not in my power to obey you, and hate him [Macheath]" (2.11). The highwaymen also offer a contrast to the ledger-book success of the Peachums: they have to leave the counting room and risk their lives for their profits, and they are in general more loyal and more generous to each other (it comes as a shock to Macheath when he discovers that one of his gang has betrayed him). Even the whores, though also with traitresses in their number, "are always so taken up with stealing hearts, that [they] don't allow [themselves] time to steal any thing else" (2.4). There is a passion driving them that is totally lacking in the calculating world of the counting house.

Handel, Walpole, and Gay:
The Aims of *The Beggar's Opera*

William A. McIntosh

> I have deferr'd writing to you from time to time till I
> could give you an account of the *Beggar's Opera*. It is
> acted at the Playhouse in Lincoln's Inn fields, with such
> success that the Playhouse hath been crowded every
> night; to night is the fifteenth time of Acting, and 'tis
> thought it will run a fortnight longer.
>
> (John Gay, 1728)

Gay's letter to Swift, written some two weeks after *The Beggar's
Opera* opened on January 29, 1728, might have seemed to some an
extraordinary boast. The expectation that his play would equal its
already unprecedented run was, however, well founded. At a time
when a dozen consecutive performances of a play were all but un-
heard of, *The Beggar's Opera* was produced without interruption no
fewer than sixty-two times. After more than a week's run (the
usual interval signaling a play's success) the *Daily Journal* reported
that at Lincoln's Inn Fields "no one third Part of the Company that
crowd thither to see [the play], can get Admittance." Even after the
close of the 1727–28 season *The Beggar's Opera* was acted an additional fifteen times at the Haymarket Theatre by a semiprofessional
company. Indeed, it was not until the 1732–33 season that audiences were drawn to *The Beggar's Opera* with promises that one
of the afterpiece's actresses would dress in boy's clothing or that

From *Eighteenth-Century Studies* 7, no. 4 (Summer 1974). © 1974 by the Regents
of the University of California.

"Signora Violante will perform her surprising Entertainments on the Rope [6 September 1732]."

The remarkable success of *The Beggar's Opera* is perhaps matched only by critical misprisions of the play. To be sure, a great deal of scholarship has gone into studies of *The Beggar's Opera,* but from our vantage point some two and a half centuries later we seem no closer to coming to grips with it than Herring, Burney, or Hawkins. The precise circumstances occasioning *The Beggar's Opera,* or the purpose of the play itself, may never be understood fully, but before any substantial answers to either of those questions can be formulated, it is necessary to clear the air—to put into proper perspective if not altogether dismiss, a number of critical assumptions which heretofore have impeded a productive study of the play. To borrow from James Sutherland: *The Beggar's Opera* "has suffered, in fact, from the most damaging kind of criticism that gives with one hand and takes away with the other." The purpose of this paper, then, is not to assert a set of conditions that led Gay to produce *The Beggar's Opera,* or even to suggest what he is up to in the play itself; instead, my intention is to scrutinize, and, where possible, to set aside the critical commonplaces that surround the play, to dispense with the notion that Gay's ostensible purpose in writing *The Beggar's Opera* was the dissolution of Handelian opera, and to open a path for subsequent studies of the play less overgrown than the one this study has had to follow.

I

A set of Quaker pastorals might succeed, if our friend Gay could fancy it, and I think it a fruitful subject; pray hear what he says. I believe farther, the pastoral ridicule is not exhausted, and that a porter, footman, or chairman's pastoral might do well. Or what think you of a Newgate pastoral among the whores and thieves there?

(Jonathan Swift, 1716)

Swift seems to have been enthusiastic about his proposal for a Newgate pastoral, and many discussions of *The Beggar's Opera* point to his suggestion as being the motivation behind the play. Few, however, take into account that Swift's letter was sent to Pope, not Gay, or that more than eleven years passed before Gay wrote *The Beggar's Opera.* In fact, according to Pope, Gay gave up the idea of a Newgate pastoral in favor of a comedy. Spence quotes Pope as saying: "This [decision of Gay's] was what gave rise to *The Beggar's Opera*. He began on it, and when first he mentioned it to Swift, the Doctor did not much like the project." The issue here is not that Swift favored the pastoral form over comedy. More to the point is that Swift was urging a variety of humor that has as its basis an unlikely turn of one kind or another. What could be more bizarre than a pastoral in which a Quaker bacchanal is celebrated, if not a picture of thieves and whores frolicking like shepherds and nymphs? It is exactly that sort of humor that prompted Swift's "Ode on a Lady's Dressing Room" in which the lovely coquette is portrayed void of any cosmetic charms and perched upon a chamber pot.

Such incongruities delighted the members of the Scriblerus Club, and one may find in the *Memoirs of Martin Scriblerus* the essential burden of *The Beggar's Opera*. In his endeavors "to find out the Seat of the Soul," Martinus discovered that

> Calves and Philosophers, Tygers and Statesmen, Foxes and Sharpers, Peacocks and Fops, Cock-Sparrows and Coquets, Monkeys and Players, Courtiers and Spaniels, Moles and Misers, exactly resemble one another in the conformation of the *Pineal Gland*. He did not doubt likewise to find the same resemblances in Highwaymen and Conquerors.

There is little difference in Martinus's record of his discoveries and the epigrammatic remarks of Gay's Beggar, who says: "Through the whole piece you may observe such a similitude of manners in high and low life, that it is difficult to determine whether (in the fashionable vices) the fine gentlemen imitate the gentlemen of the road, or the gentlemen of the road the fine gentlemen." The comic ethos amounts to a portrayal of the incongruous, the antecedents of which have some peripheral relationship to Swift's suggestion of a Newgate pastoral, but less tenuous is the play's connection with the Scriblerian activity of 1726–27.

All of that is not to imply *The Beggar's Opera* was not prompted by other considerations, but it should, if nothing else, evoke a more cautious approach to critics such as Hawkins, who reduces the occasioning of the play to a purely personal level. Of Gay, Sir John writes: "The motive for writing the piece, and for

the many acrimonious expressions and bitter invectives against
statesmen, lawyers, priests, and others, contained in it, was the disappointment of Mr. Gay in his application for preferment at
court." But Gay was capable of the same sorts of analogies Hawkins refers to long before he lost his place at court. In late summer
of 1723 Gay wrote the following to Mrs. Howard:

> I cannot indeed wonder that the Talents requisite for a
> great Statesman are so scarce in the world since so many
> of those who possess them are every month cut off in the
> prime of their age at the Old Baily. How envious are
> Statesmen! and how jealous are they of rivals! A High-
> way-man never picks up an honest man for a companion,
> but if such a one accidentally falls his way; if he cannot
> turn his heart He like a wise Statesman discards him. An-
> other observation I have made upon Courtiers, is, that if
> you have any friendship with any particular one you
> must be entirely governed by his friendships and resent-
> ments not your own.

More than four years passed before Gay's hopes for an important
position at court were dashed by his appointment as Gentleman-
usher to the two-year-old Princess Louisa. After declining the post
he wrote to Swift, "As I am us'd to disappointments I can bear
them, but as I can have no more hopes, I can no more be disappointed, so that I am in a blessed condition." Though Gay's tone
is not one of delight, it suggests a kind of resignation, and nothing
more. Nor does Swift's reply to his friend. He writes, "I entirely
approve your refusal of that employment, and your writing to the
Queen. I am perfectly confident that you have a firm enemy in the
Ministry [viz., Walpole]. God forgive him, but not till he puts himself in a state to be forgiven."

Gay, remember, had finished *The Beggar's Opera* sometime in
October of 1727, which, we see, was a crucial period in his political
life. It seems unlikely indeed that a man who had hopes of obtain-
ing a significant position at court would jeopardize his chances by
insulting the one man who could help him. His friendship with the
Scriblerians would have made his political life difficult enough
without his taking up the torch against the Ministry. One might
argue that to ease his spleen Gay revised *The Beggar's Opera* after
losing the appointment, but time has to be taken into account. *The*

Beggar's Opera is not simply another eighteenth-century comedy—though without its music the play might pass for one easily enough—but instead a fairly complex dramatic piece that required some degree of musical collaboration, and more important, rehearsal. At the very latest it would have had to have been to Rich by the new year, and before that some time was lost when Gay took the play to Cibber. In short, Gay had perhaps less than two months to alter the play, and, as will be discussed more fully in another section of this paper, if any alteration did take place it was to weaken, not intensify, the sting of *The Beggar's Opera*.

To summarize, then, the play seems to have been occasioned by Gay's desire to produce a comedy of incongruities, built around his long-held notion of the impingement of the rapacious and base on polite society. That Gay would draw the parallels he does between high and low life is no surprise; nor is his opting for a dramatic vehicle. What does remain puzzling, however, is the dramatic form he chose.

Many commentators take Gay's use of the ballad opera as an explicit jab at Italian opera in general, and Handelian opera in particular. That question is discussed fully in the following section, but there can be no doubt whatever that Gay's selection of a musical mode was influenced by the immense popularity of Italian opera. There was, however, a long tradition of the use of dramatic song on the English stage from which Gay must have drawn; indeed, his use of music in *The Beggar's Opera* more closely matches Shakespeare's in *The Tempest* than either of *The Tempest's* revisions set by Purcell and Arne. Nor was Gay the first to bring a ballad opera to the eighteenth-century theatre. There are at least three plays produced earlier in the century that may be classified as ballad operas. Of those, Gay's play has greatest kinship with Thomas D'Urfey's *Wonders in the Sun* (1706). Burney records that D'Urfey's play ran for five nights before closing, which was a satisfactory performance record, if a disappointment to D'Urfey. Gay could expect a comparable run for his own play for novelty's sake alone. His friends were not so confident. According to Spence, Pope, speaking for himself and Swift, remarked: "When it was done neither of us thought it would succeed. We showed it to Congreve, who, after reading it over, said, 'It would either take greatly, or be damned confoundly.' "

The motivation behind Gay's writing a ballad opera may never be plumbed, nor can the reasons for its staggering success compared with the barely adequate run of D'Urfey's ballad opera be understood completely. Of one thing we can be certain: Both the comic ethos and the dramatic form of *The Beggar's Opera* number Gay among the great wits of the eighteenth century. As Dr. Johnson so aptly observed: "Whether this new drama was the product of judgment or luck, the praise of it must be given to the inventor."

II

In the year 1727, Violent Parties were formed, between the 2 famous Singers, Faustina and Cuzzoni; and in the Election for Directors Faustina's Party carried it. These Animosities were very prejudicial to the Interest of the Academy, and the Houses began to grow thinner upon it. *The Beggar's Opera* appearing soon after, gave such a Turn to the Town, that Operas were generally neglected.

(The Earl of Shaftesbury, 1760)

Charles Burney quotes Cromwell as saying that Italian opera, "being in an unintelligible tongue . . . cannot corrupt the morals of the People," but owing to its absolute power on the English stage during the first three decades of the eighteenth century, it managed, as Shaftesbury implies, to corrupt itself absolutely. The rivalries between singers, the castrati, flamboyant and idiotic props, libretti of the most pathetic sort, and a host of other absurdities elicited growing sentiments against the opera that ranged from the amusing, if highly subjective, satires of Addison to the gloomy declamation of Arthur Bedford. Gay was no less aware of the foibles of Italian opera than the rest of London, and the entirety of *The Beggar's Opera* is filled with satiric barbs directed at it. But most critics who have not taken Dr. Johnson's remark that "this play [is] written in ridicule of the musical Italian drama," as sufficient comment have gone off on tangents of ingenuity that all but blast Gay out of the water.

Those critics who have fantasized an enmity between Handel and Gay, or even an intense hatred for Italian opera on Gay's part, not only have failed to understand Gay's play, but also have distorted historical fact. It has been observed elsewhere that there is no evidence to suggest that Handel was annoyed with Gay after the appearance of *The Beggar's Opera*. In fact, there is considerable evidence to show that Handel was not upset, and even more to demonstrate the existence of a pleasant association of that great master and the Scriblerians. There is nothing in the writings or letters of Handel that indicates he was smarting from Gay's "attack," and it is interesting to note that he had entered into a new partnership with "gay" John Rich by August of 1734. During the early 1720s Handel, Gay, Pope, and Arbuthnot had all gathered at Canons with the Duke of Chandos, and apparently that company was an harmonious one. One late-eighteenth-century writer records their relationship thus:

> [Pope] heard the performances of Handel with perfect indifference, if not impatience. Gay was pleased with music without understanding it, but forgot the performance when the notes ceased to vibrate. Arbuthnot, on the contrary, who was a judge of music, and a composer, felt the merits of Handel, and conceived an esteem of him, which he afterwards displayed under the most trying circumstances.
>
> (John Christopher Smith, 1799)

Handel's association with Gay's circle had begun a decade before the Canons period. Aaron Hill, Gay's friend and classmate under Robert Luck, approached Handel with the idea of *Rinaldo,* and it was at Hill's instance and under his supervision that Paolo Rolli completed the libretto that Handel set. Some five years later, in 1716, Gay's *Trivia* recalled his time with Handel and the others at Burlington's palace:

> There *Hendel* strikes the Strings, the melting Strain
> Transports the Soul, and thrills through ev'ry Vein;
> There oft' I enter (but with cleaner Shoes)
> For *Burlington's* belov'd by ev'ry Muse.

In 1719 Handel brought out his first setting of Gay's masque, *Acis and Galatea,* and the following year, along with his partner in opera, Heidegger, he was among the subscribers to Gay's poems. It was also in 1720 that Handel completed his first English oratorio, *Esther.* When it was performed at Canons on August 29 of that year, the audience heard Handel's settings of airs written for *Esther* by Arbuthnot, Pope, and Gay. During the 1725 revival of *The What D'Ye Call It,* Handel's " 'Twas When the Seas Were Roaring" was performed, and he was delighted when Gay used it again in *The Beggar's Opera*. Perhaps most telling of all is this exchange between Pepusch and Handel, recorded by Hibbert after *The Beggar's Opera* was produced:

> PEPUSCH: I hope, sir, you do not include me among'st
> those who did injustice to your talents.
> HANDEL: Nod at all, nod at all, God forbid! I am a great
> admirer of the airs of *The Beggar's Opera,* and every
> professional gentleman must do his best to live.

Handel is not being magnanimous; nor should he have been. An opera, even a ballad opera, drawing together the works of Purcell, Clarke, Bononcini, Eccles, would have been remiss to have excluded Handel's.

It has been argued that Gay's attack on opera was merely another manifestation of his difficulties at court—that because opera enjoyed the support of the crown Gay felt it had to be destroyed. Such a circumstance is unlikely indeed. And even if the assertion were correct, it should be noted that Handel's difficulties with the court were very much like Gay's. He was actively and viciously opposed by the Prince of Wales for several years, and by 1729, Hawkins reports, was himself completely at odds with the court.

Those who supported opera, and particularly that of Handel, continued their support despite the growing canon of ballad operas. Handel was not at all put off by the appearances of his music in *Polly,* 1729, as evinced by his subscription to Gay's collected works in 1730. Nor was he deterred from reviving *Rinaldo* in 1731. For a form which was supposed to have been driven from the stage, composed by a man who was supposed to have been forced away from opera, *Rinaldo* did remarkably well. It was performed at the Haymarket Theatre no fewer than six times in less than a month. Finally, and significantly, Handel continued, after its initial London performance in 1731, to revive *Acis and Galatea,* "which in every Respect charms, to this Day, Persons of all Ranks and Capacities," up to his death in 1759. That Handel gave up the composition of opera is undeniable, but that the appearances of *The Beggar's Opera, Polly, Achilles,* or any of the others were responsible is as untenable as the assertion that John Gay led the crusade out of animus toward a man who had been his friend for two decades.

Among recent commentators, C. F. Burgess is perhaps most

adamant in his arguments that Gay was militantly against Italian opera. Gay's oft quoted letter is frequently cited as evidence of his antipathy toward opera, and it is worth looking at again here. On February 3, 1722/23, he writes to Swift:

> As for the reigning Amusement of the town, tis entirely Musick. Real fiddles, Bass Vials [sic] and Hautboys not Poetical Harps, Lyres, and reeds. Theres [sic] nobody allow'd to say I sing but an Eunuch or an Italian Woman. Every body is grown now as great a judge of Musick as they were in your time of Poetry. And folks that could not distinguish one tune from another now daily dispute about the different styles of Hendel, Bononcini, and Attillo. People have now forgot Homer, and Virgil & Caesar, or at least they have lost their ranks, for in London and Westminster in all polite conversation's Senesino is daily voted to be the greatest man that ever liv'd.

A close reading of that passage suggests that Gay is talking about people, not music. His sarcasm is leveled at the "great judges" of music *and* poetry; moreover, he is concerned here with the fickle nature of polite society, not with that society's longing for opera. Swift's views are another matter altogether; however, it is important to remember that Swift, not Gay, wrote:

> [*The Beggar's Opera*] likewise exposeth with Great Justice that unnatural Taste for Italian Musick among us, which is wholly unsuitable to our Northern Climate, and the Genius of the People, whereby we are overrun with Italian-Effeminacy, and Italian Nonsense.

That is not to say that Gay was not disgusted with certain features of the opera. Any sensible and sensitive person must have been. But the passage extracted from his letter to Swift is his most fully developed comment on the subject of opera, excepting *The Beggar's Opera,* and that will carry the argument only so far.

Addison's four *Spectator* essays have also been cited as proof of Gay's opposition to Italian opera. First, it must be remembered that the most recent of Addison's attacks was printed on April 3, 1711, scarcely more than a month after the triumphal opening of *Rinaldo.* Four years earlier Addison had been humiliated by the financial and artistic disaster of his own opera, *Rosamond.* None of that, however, has anything whatsoever to do with John Gay. When *The Beggar's Opera* was written, Addison had been dead for some eight years. Further, it is not certain that Steele shared Addison's vehement feelings against the new opera; none of the four *Spectator* numbers in question bears Steele's mark. And there is no reason to believe that Steele, even granting that he agreed with Addison, urged them on Gay. He was not one of Gay's intimates, and at the time *The Beggar's Opera* came to the stage was, himself, ill.

That Gay hated the foreignness of Italian opera is a misconception at best; at worst it is the result of putting Swift's words into Gay's mouth. If the foreign flavor of the opera is what bothered Gay, how ironic it is that he should bring to the English stage a variety of the German *Singspiel*. Excepting only those done by Carey, every ballad opera, including *The Beggar's Opera,* was arranged and orchestrated by a German. Perhaps even more ironic is that the intentionally simple English melodies of *The Beggar's Opera* were to become bravura concert pieces that grew more florid with each production of the play. Burney laments:

> But either from the ambition of the singer, or expectations of the audience, Music is not suffered to remain simple long upon the stage; and the more plain and ancient the melodies, the more they are to be embellished by every new performer of them. The tunes in *The Beggar's Opera* will never appear in their original simple garb again.

From Burney's comments, then, it would seem that the actions of ballad opera stars had become mirrors of Faustina and Cuzzoni, or, if not, that the audiences became not unlike those that flocked to Covent Garden and Haymarket for the opera. Perhaps it was the good fortune of Gay, Swift, and even Handel to have been laid to rest before a Dublin revival of *The Beggar's Opera* on January 2, 1765. The part of the swaggering Macheath was taken by Ann Catley, but to make matters worse, all the music had been "newly improved" and ornamented by a young Italian composer, Tommaso Giordani.

There is a tradition that on the opening night of *The Beggar's Opera* the audience took Pepusch's overture to be the first sounding, but when no second music was forthcoming, the audience all but lost control. To silence the crowd, the comedian Jack Hall was sent out to explain that there would be no further soundings, but the hush that fell over the audience when he appeared so unnerved him that he blurted out: "Ladies and Gentlemen, we—we beg you will not call for First and Second Music, bec-because you know—there is never any music at all to an opera." Perhaps it was Jack Hall's *faux pas* that began the whole gruesome tradition of reading *The Beggar's Opera* as a brutal satire designed to destroy Italian opera. Surely Gay never intended to do more than offer, as Bukofzer wisely suggests [in *Music in the Baroque Era*], a few good humored parodies for the amusement of the friends of *opera seria*. Given the sorts of straws that have been grasped by some, one wonders why someone has not attempted to establish a link between the cage of sparrows Addison lampoons in the fifth *Spectator* and the over thirty references to birds, beginning with Polly's name, that Gay includes in his play. The point, simply, is this: if lampoon is to be appreciated it must first be recognizable. The Lucy-Polly conflict may very well allude to the bickerings of Faustina and Cuzzoni. Or does it, as many have suggested, recall a quarrel (of which there is no record) between Lady Walpole and Maria Skerrett, Sir Robert's mistress? If one must choose, the former is certainly the more plausible. Notwithstanding the assertion that *everyone* knew of Walpole's philandering, the prime minister never took it to the stage; Faustina and Cuzzoni, quite literally, aired their linen before the public, and few in Gay's audience would have failed to make the connection between the two famous singers and the play's two female leads. But that sort of parody hardly constitutes a vicious attack on opera; moreover, those who followed opera were not charmed with the antics of the two prima donnas, and would have been as pleased with the joke as a Jonathan Swift.

If Gay had wanted opera off the stage he would not have relied merely upon a singers' war, or the speeches of the beggar at the beginning and end of the play for they are too subtle. Such techniques almost always produce laughter, but rarely do they produce anger. If the death of opera was Gay's goal, he could have secured it easily enough. Macheath, instead of a rich tenor, could have been played by a squeaking castrato; Peachum, instead of dealing in contraband would have kidnapped young boys for the opera; Gay might have demanded the same sort of musical treatment of his songs from Pepusch as they actually received from Giordani four decades later. But Gay did none of those things. There are swipes at opera in his play, but swipes are not death blows. To look for more is to spoil the fun; to see more is to see something that does not exist.

III

Does Walpole think you intended an affront to him in your opera? Pray God he may, for he has held the longest hand at hazard that ever fell to any sharper's share, and keeps his run when the dice are changed.

(Jonathan Swift, 1728)

One of the most significant contributions to the study of Walpole's being satirized in *The Beggar's Opera* was made some years ago by Jean Kern, who ends once and for all the myth that the Peachum-Lockit quarrel is a parody of a similar disagreement between Walpole and his brother-in-law, Townshend. The Walpole-Townshend row, if anything, was a parody of the quarrel that had been acted out on stage more than a year before. Walpole is among the targets of the play's satire, but the extent to which he is ridiculed must, as Professor Kern's example suggests, be approached with some caution. Gay did not, in fact, nurture a long hatred for Walpole, and from the presence of his name on the list of Gay's subscribers in 1720 it seems that the prime minister was nominally cordial toward Gay.

Walpole, of course, was not a beloved figure, and it is well known that the first organized opposition to him can be traced to the Scriblerian activities of the period 1726–29. I have already established that Gay had sufficient reason to be at odds with Walpole by 1727, but he was no fool and not about to risk a head-on collision with so powerful an adversary. Even Walpole could tolerate the references to himself in "Robin of Bagshot, alias Gorgon, alias Bluff Bob, alias Carbuncle, alias Bob Booty," and there are numerous reports of his calling for an encore of the air (30) that ends with the line: "That was levelled at me." What he could not tolerate, though, would be an allusion to his dalliances. And if the Polly-Lucy argument is intended to embarrass Walpole, how cleverly Gay has covered himself. The obvious analogue is the operatic rivalry, and it is behind that similarity Gay could take refuge. If the burden of *The Beggar's Opera* is an attack on the Walpole government, it necessarily must have been camouflaged; and what better subterfuge than the burlesque of an opera?

In the amount of criticism received, opera was second only to the Ministry; Handel, second only to Walpole. And the association between the two men, at least as far as the public could tell, was strong. On three occasions it was Walpole who arranged pensions for Handel, though neither man held any affection for the other. As late as 1733, well after Handel's rift with the court, they were connected in print. On June 15, 1733, *The Craftsman* carried this epigram:

> Quoth W———e to H———l, shall We Two agree,
> and Excise the whole Nation?
> [Handel:] Si, caro, Si.
> Of what use are Sheep if the Shepherds can't sheer them
> At the Haymarket I, you at Westminster?
> [Walpole:] Hear him.
> Call'd to order, the seconds appear'd in their place;
> One fam'd for his Morals, and one for his Face.
> In half they succeed, in half they were crost:
> The Excise was obtained, but poor *Deborah* lost.

If the orientation of *The Beggar's Opera* is political, there are, subterfuge notwithstanding, few substantial allusions to Walpole. The Peachum-Lockit parallel does not exist; the Polly-Lucy conflict is tenuous at best. More to the point, perhaps, is the parody of Walpole's having to choose between his wife and mistress in Macheath's "How Happy Could I Be with Either" (air 35), but even that would have meaning to only a very few. Gay's allusion in Robin of Bagshot is transparent, but there is never the sort of clearly defined allegorical schema to the play that allows positive identifications to be made.

It has been noted that the mode of political satire is established by the overture before the play ever begins. Pepusch incorporated into his overture a tune known as "Walpole." That title was not so well known as an earlier one, "The Happy Clown," and when the same tune appears in *The Beggar's Opera* as "I'm Like a Skiff on the Ocean Tossed" (air 47), it is printed under its original and best known title, "One Evening Having Lost My Way." When Lucy sings the air, it is set in G major with a time signature of 6/8. The overture, however, is written in the key of B-flat major with a time signature of 12/8. First, it is unlikely that the audience ever heard the overture through its own din; second, it is doubtful that the air would have been recognized, for Pepusch treats it in fugal form in the allegro section of his French overture, and the tempo, even when the tonic melody can be followed, is considerably faster than the tempo at which it was supposed to have been sung. Only a trained musician could have recognized the melody in the amount of time it took the orchestra to play it, and an extraordinary pair of ears would have been needed to have heard it played at all on the two oboes, two violins, and harpsichord for which that part of the overture was scored.

Taken altogether, the political satire of the play is hardly so potent as to conclude that it brought about Walpole's downfall. Gay no more had that in mind than the dissolution of Italian opera. It was Swift who saw Walpole as damned, not Gay, whose own views, like those of Pope, were mixed; "both lunched with and satirized Sir Robert" (Armens). Gay had been hurt, but not to the point of wanting to destroy himself, and to have gone farther than all concrete evidence indicates he went would have spelled his end. Even so, it seems he struck closer to home than he had intended, or, perhaps, the joke simply had worn itself out. Despite the façade of good cheer, one cannot but pity the writer of these lines:

> By the beginning of my letter you see how I decline in favour, but I look upon it as my particular distinction, that as soon as the Court gains a man I lose him; tis a mortification I have been us'd to, so I bear it as a philosopher should.

IV

> But the best of all was Sir William Ashurst, who sat in a box, and was perhaps one of the first judges who ever figured away at *The Beggar's Opera,* that strong and bitter satire against the professions, and particularly his.
>
> (Hannah More, 1778)

More studies of *The Beggar's Opera* would do well to take up Sir William's standard, for it is in its treatment of the professions, especially law, that the play's most pointed and consistent satire exists. Exactly what Gay is attempting, or why he is attempting it, remains a mystery. Hawkins's suggestion, which was quoted earlier, seems to be off the mark, as do the many that have followed it. No one has taken into account the tradition of legal satire carried on by the later Jacobean and Caroline playwrights for the benefit of their Inns of Court coterie. Nor has there been any explanation for Gay's dark, almost twentieth-century view of humanity. Certainly that was the feature of the play that attracted Brecht's attention.

On no fewer than eleven occasions there are explicit references that call the legal profession into question (act 1, sc. 1, 2, 4, 9, 13; and airs 1, 2, 11, 24, 57, 67). Each of those is put into the mouth of one of the play's low-life figures, as if some sort of vindication through balance and antithesis were intended. Every vile act in the play is justified by the vilification of polite society or one of the professions.

> The gamesters and lawyers are jugglers alike
> If they meddle, your all is in danger:

sings Jenny Diver to Macheath an instant before giving him the Judas-like kiss that allows him to be taken off in chains. Peachum's masterminding of the release of several members of his gang is followed by Filch's air, which observes:

> For suits of love, like law, are won by pay
> And beauty must be fee'd into our arms.

Peachum and his wife plot the undoing of Macheath, and that is sealed with an air containing these lines:

> If lawyer's hand is fee'd, sir,
> He steals your whole estate.

And the pattern repeats itself time and again throughout the play.

The morality of the play, or lack of it, prompted a number of attacks, most famous of which was Bishop Herring's sermon against *The Beggar's Opera*. If only for its splendid polemic, a portion of Swift's answer to the Bishop is worth quoting. "Upon the whole," he writes,

> I deliver my judgment That nothing but servile Attachment to a Party, Affectation of Singularity, lamentable Dullness, mistaken Zeal, or studied Hypocrisy, can have the least reasonable Objection against this excellent moral Performance of the Celebrated Mr. Gay.

In fact, Swift never answers the critics of the play's morality; perhaps he dared not. The world of Gay's play is a world of enormities, but so, too, is the world that watches it. After the rabble has cried its reprieve, the beggar steps forward and remarks:

> Had the play remained as I first intended, it would have
> carried a most excellent moral. 'Twould have shown that
> the lower sort of people have their vices in a degree as
> well as the rich, and that they are punished for them.
>
> (act 3, sc. 16)

Like the beggar, we know that there is no morality in the liberation
of Macheath, but like Gay, we know too that there is no morality
in his being hanged by men who belong on the scaffold with him.
Gay does not, like almost all his contemporaries in drama, give us
romp, which is tied up by the meting out of a brand of inefficacious
poetic justice in the last scene. *The Beggar's Opera* is no thesis play,
but neither is it mere frolic. Gay wants to entertain, and in that he
succeeds most excellently. But if his treatment of society and the
professions evokes laughter, it also evokes a feeling of uneasiness
among those laughing. We are placed in the uncomfortable position
of having to come to terms with two worlds. The world within the
play is crowded with criminals on every level, but so is the world
without. What we do with that second world is our own affair.
What Gay himself would have done with it—indeed, what he already had done with it—is manifestly obvious in his letters.

In the preceding pages I have discussed the events and attitudes
that occasioned *The Beggar's Opera,* set aside the notion that the aim
of the play was the dissolution of Italian opera, and suggested a
more cautious view of the play's political satire. I have suggested
that the dominant force in *The Beggar's Opera* is its professional and
social satire, and that its function is essentially didactic. Finally, I
have implied that in working toward a stage didactic that proffers
something other than pap, Gay is unique among his contemporaries. This paper does not pretend to do more than open the door to
subsequent investigations, whose starting point should not be with
the tired clichés put away here, but instead with a kind of drama
unique in its time, the work of "a natural man, without design,
who spoke what he thought, and just as he thought it (Alexander
Pope on John Gay).

The Beggar's Opera as Opera and Anti-opera

Peter Lewis

It must be allow'd an Opera in all its forms.

Today *The Beggar's Opera* is usually regarded as one of the very few great English plays of the eighteenth century and as one of the major literary works of the Augustan period; yet the title asserts unequivocally that it is an opera. This apparent discrepancy poses the question—what kind of opera? To Gay's contemporaries, the title of his work would at first have seemed as incongruous (although for a slightly different reason) as those of the mock-heroic poems. *The Rape of the Lock* and *The Dunciad,* by his friend Pope. Writing for an elite educated in the classics, Pope knew that the words "The Rape of" would bring to mind "The Rape of Leda" or "The Rape of Helen" or "The Rape of Lucretia," myths and stories about events that had wide-ranging repercussions of epic proportions, such as the Trojan War. "The Rape of" produces expectations that are dashed by the rest of Pope's title referring to a lock of hair. Similarly *The Dunciad* recalls Homer's *Iliad* and Virgil's *Aeneid,* but Pope's title indicates that his poem is an inverted epic, not of heroes but of dunces. By the time Gay wrote *The Beggar's Opera* in 1727, "opera" in England had become virtually synonymous with Italian opera, a theatrical form characterized by great dignity and seriousness and peopled with mythological figures or personages of high rank from the distant past. That an "opera" could be a "beggar's"

From *John Gay: The Beggar's Opera.* © 1976 by Peter Lewis. E. Arnold, 1976.

consequently amounted to a contradiction in terms. Gay's very title more or less announces that he is turning Italian opera upside down, that his own opera is both a burlesque of the Italian form and a radically new kind of English opera, indeed the first comic opera, since before Gay most operas were devoid of levity and none sported such a flippant and unlikely title as *The Beggar's Opera*.

In order to appreciate the rationale behind Gay's opera, it is necessary to know something about the history of opera in England during the preceding three-quarters of a century. Toward the end of the Interregnum, it was possible to get round the Puritan ban on the staging of plays by presenting in private houses dramatic works which featured musical accompaniment throughout. These established a form, the English dramatic opera, that survived the reopening of the theatres in 1660 following the restoration of the monarchy. After 1660, however, there was no need for the music to be sustained throughout in order to evade prosecution, and the all-sung pattern of the Interregnum operas, in which every word had to be set to music, was abandoned. In form, though not of course in content, the dramatic opera of the Restoration period resembles the modern musical more closely than modern opera, which derives from Italian opera. The music is intermittent rather than continuous and some of the dialogue is spoken rather than sung, but the musical sections, although embedded within the framework of a spoken play, are usually much more important than the nonmusical sections. As far as content goes, on the other hand, English dramatic opera resembles Italian opera in that the world it presents is elevated and heroic rather than realistic. Early in the eighteenth century the popularity of dramatic opera waned, and even though a few English operas continued to hold the stage after 1710, the genre was rapidly supplanted by Italian opera.

Not long after the 1705 production of *Arsinoe,* the first Italianate opera to be staged in England, a vogue for Italian opera was developing. What did more than anything else to accelerate this development was Handel's visit to London in 1710 and his subsequent decision to stay there. Handel, a prolific composer of genius but also something of an opportunist, arrived at exactly the right time. He was immediately commissioned to write an Italian opera and obliged with *Rinaldo* (1711), the first of many popular successes he supplied to English audiences. From 1710 the new Queen's Theatre was the home of Italian opera in England and became known as the Opera House. Furthermore, leading Italian singers were paid enormous sums to perform in London and, as "stars," were figures of widespread public interest. In the year in which *The Beggar's Opera* was written, for example, the personal feud between the two leading ladies of Italian opera in London, Faustina Bordoni and Francesca Cuzzoni, provided a considerable amount of offstage entertainment, especially as on one occasion it erupted on stage into mutual punching, scratching and hair-pulling.

The snobbish vogue for Italian opera and the idolizing of its principal performers soon produced a hostile reaction from some English intellectuals, who laughed at the male castrati singers, at the temperamental behaviour of the prima donnas, at the convention of recitative, at the lavishness of operatic productions, and at the fact that operas were sung in a language which was incomprehensible to most of the audience. To some extent such mockery can be put down to patriotic bias, but neoclassical critics like Addison and Dennis genuinely believed that the vogue for Italian opera posed a threat to the orthodox dramatic forms of tragedy and comedy as well as to the vitality of English music. One of the charges levelled against Italian opera was that its appeal was very superficial, delighting the ear and the eye but failing to supply the intellectual stimulus and spiritual nourishment afforded by the English dramatic tradition since the Elizabethans.

Gay himself was musical and did not dislike Italian opera in the way that his more doctrinaire neoclassical contemporaries did. Indeed, he even provided Handel with an operatic libretto, *Acis and Galatea,* about ten years before he wrote *The Beggar's Opera.* But during the 1720s he became alarmed at the ever-increasing popularity of Italian opera and its effect on English drama and music. "As for the reigning Amusement of the town, tis entirely Musick," he complains in a letter to Swift (February 3, 1723), adding that "folks that could not distinguish one tune from another now daily dispute about the different Styles of Hendel, Bononcini, and Attillio." Just as Jane Austen objected much less to the Gothic novel per se than to the excessive seriousness with which it was taken by impressionable members of the reading public, Gay condemns not Italian opera but the completely uncritical theatregoers who had turned it into a fashionable cult. Jane Austen nevertheless felt that a corrective was necessary, and in *Northanger Abbey* wrote a book that is both a burlesque of Gothic fiction and a realistic novel in its own right. In conceiving *The Beggar's Opera* Gay did something very similar. He set out to combine burlesque of Italian opera with the creation of a rival form, a comic and distinctly English form of opera that quickly became known as ballad opera. This dual purpose explains the considerable difference between *The Beggar's Opera* and the few previous burlesques of Italian opera, which are aimed at very specific targets and do not attempt to transcend burlesque. Gay deliberately avoids direct parody and close burlesque because this might well have prevented him from achieving a self-sufficient "opera" capable of standing as an independent work of art.

Musically, there are two great differences between *The Beggar's Opera* and Italian opera. Firstly, much of Gay's work consists of orthodox dramatic dialogue without any musical accompaniment, whereas all the words in Italian opera are sung; in this respect *The Beggar's Opera* resembles the English dramatic opera of the Restoration more closely than Italian opera. Secondly, apart from the overture, the music for *The Beggar's Opera* was taken from preexisting sources, whereas an Italian opera was an entirely new musical creation. For the sixty-nine songs in the play, Gay himself selected the melodies, most of which were well known. Forty-one of the airs have broadside-ballad tunes (this explains the term "ballad opera") but others have tunes by such distinguished contemporary composers as Purcell and Handel; air 22 is actually sung to the music of a march in one of Handel's greatest operatic successes, *Rinaldo*. What Gay did—and this was his most daringly original stroke—was to put new wine into old bottles, substituting his own words for the familiar ones, though retaining and modifying phrases here and there. This gamble might have failed disastrously, but Gay did it so well that in no time at all dramatic hacks were churning out inferior imitations. In the years immediately following 1728, ballad operas and ballad farces darkened the air; and although Italian opera continued to be popular, it now had to compete with a new vogue. Whatever Gay may have thought of the progeny his masterpiece spawned, he had certainly succeeded in restoring English opera. Today "opera" seems the wrong word, but in the case of *The Beggar's Opera,* the large number of songs together with their vital dramatic importance distinguish it from plays of the seventeenth and early eighteenth centuries containing incidental music and songs. There is nothing incidental about Gay's memorable songs, and to many people they are the glory of the work.

As has been noted, Gay's burlesque of Italian opera is for the most part indirect and nonparodic, but his burlesque purpose explains many features of *The Beggar's Opera*. In order to maintain a superficial resemblance to Italian opera, Gay adopts several of its formal characteristics, such as a three-act structure instead of the five-act structure invariable in full-length tragedies and comedies. Again, following the example of Italian opera and departing from the customary practice of orthodox drama, he dispenses with both prologue and epilogue, the conventional and completely detachable speeches preceding and following a tragedy or comedy that were often contributed by someone other than the author. Operas did not open with a prologue but with an instrumental overture, and Gay specifies that an overture should be played for *The Beggar's Opera*. For the first production, J. C. Pepusch, a German composer of theatre music, provided a suitable overture featuring the melody Gay chose for air 47. Although Gay's use of speech instead of recitative is a significant departure from operatic practice, his actual layout of the airs corresponds to that of arias in an Italian opera. The sudden switching from speech to song and back again without any attempt to justify the interpolation of an air on realistic grounds, as is often done in orthodox drama, recalls the alternation of recitatives and arias in opera. There is a further correspondence to Italian opera in that not all of Gay's airs are solos, some being duets, one being a trio, and a few involving a chorus.

Gay goes to some pains to draw attention to these and other operatic parallels in his introduction, which precedes the overture and which is an essential part of his design in a way that the conventional prologue was not. In this short scene, the supposed author of the opera, the Beggar, explains his work to one of the actors, the Player, and claims that although written to celebrate the marriage of two English ballad singers it is to all intents and purposes an orthodox opera. Instead of announcing explicitly in his own voice that he is about to burlesque Italian opera, Gay chooses the much subtler satiric method, perfected by Swift, of adopting a "mask" or "persona," that of the Beggar, and speaking indirectly through him. The Beggar's seriousness is really Gay's sleight of hand; his words are undermined from within so that we do not take them at their face value. Gay's irony can be fully appreciated only in the light of what is to follow, but his gibe at Italian opera is unmistakable when the Beggar says, "I hope I may be forgiven, that

I have not made my Opera throughout unnatural, like those in vogue; for I have no Recitative." The Beggar appears to be apologizing for not making his opera "throughout unnatural," but by implication these words carry their own qualification and disapproval. Gay is clearly invoking the Augustan aesthetic yardstick of nature as a measure for exposing the limitations of Italian opera. The further implication that "Recitative" in particular is unnatural is a complaint often levelled against Italian opera at the time. According to Addison, English audiences were at first "wonderfully surprized to hear Generals singing the Word of Command, and Ladies delivering Messages in Musick" (*The Spectator*, no. 29).

The rest of the Beggar's speech can also be interpreted at two levels. He is pleased with himself for using "the Similes that are in all your celebrated Operas," and the ones he lists do appear in *The Beggar's Opera:* "The Swallow" in air 34, "the Moth" in air 4, "the Bee" and "the Flower" in both air 6 and air 15, and "the Ship" in both air 10 and air 47. What Gay implies, however, is that such similes have been rendered inexpressive in Italian opera by having been worked to death; after all, they are "in all your celebrated Operas," which is more or less true since simile arias were exceedingly popular. Gay himself tries to revitalize them, to rinse them clean, by employing them in an unconventional context. The Beggar also seems to be proud of his "Prison Scene which the Ladies always reckon charmingly pathetick." As his words suggest, a prison scene was almost a sine qua non in an Italian opera and usually occurred at a high point of the dramatic action so that as much emotional appeal as possible could be wrung from it. The irony here lies in the fact that not just one poignant scene but almost half of *The Beggar's Opera* takes place in a prison, and in addition that the prison is not some historically or geographically remote one with romantic associations, but Newgate prison in the heart of London, exactly as it was at the time with all its petty corruptions and abuses. As regards "the Parts," the Beggar's self-congratulation at achieving "a nice Impartiality to our two Ladies, that it is impossible for either of them to take Offence" carries a more immediately topical irony, referring as it does to the current quarrel between Francesca Cuzzoni and Faustina Bordoni over operatic roles. In some Italian operas there are two heroines who are rivals for the hero's affections, and to avoid causing friction, composers like Handel had to ensure that there was no obvious imbalance between the two parts. Nevertheless, even if they could not actually "take Offence," Francesca Cuzzoni and Faustina Bordoni tended to treat an opera in which they appeared together as a singing contest, vying with each other vocally instead of working as part of a team. This satirical reference to the prima donnas also serves to draw attention to the operatic parallel: *The Beggar's Opera* itself has two heroines, Polly Peachum and Lucy Lockit, who are rivals for the affections of the hero, Macheath. Indeed the rivalry between Polly and Lucy alludes to that of the prima donnas and to that of the operatic roles they performed.

The Beggar claims that except for using speech instead of recitative his work "must be allow'd an Opera in all its forms"; but by means of irony and by explicit references to beggars, to ballad singers, who were not particularly reputable, and to the notorious London parish of St Giles-in-the-Fields, the resort of thieves, highwaymen and prostitutes, Gay indicates throughout the introduction that the content of *The Beggar's Opera* is totally unlike that of Italian opera. While in many respects Gay does adhere to the "forms" of Italian opera, the world he presents is the very unoperatic one of St Giles-in-the-Fields. He completely inverts Italian opera, with its classical, mythological or similarly elevated narratives and its exotic atmosphere, by setting *The Beggar's Opera* very firmly in the criminal underworld of contemporary London. Theatregoers in 1728 would have recognized immediately that two of the major characters, Peachum and Macheath, were based on the best known underworld figures of the early eighteenth century, Jonathan Wild and Jack Sheppard, both of whom had been executed less than four years before the first production of the work. One of the locations is the city's principal criminal prison, and death by hanging or transportation to the colonies is the fate that seems to await most of the characters. For them, the year is divided not into seasons but into the various sessions of the city's criminal court, the Old Bailey. Instead of a typical operatic hero such as Handel's Rinaldo, Gay provides the leader of a gang of highwaymen, Macheath, who is called "Captain" but has no legitimate claim to the rank. And instead of two typical operatic heroines like the high-born Rossane and Lisaura in *Alessandro,* the opera which Handel wrote for Faustina Bordoni's London debut in 1726, Gay supplies Polly Peachum, the daughter of an organizer of crime and a receiver of stolen goods, and Lucy Lockit, the daughter of the very corrupt chief jailor of Newgate. The sustained tussle between Polly and Lucy over Macheath is a low-life equivalent of that between Rossane and Lisaura over Alessandro (Alexander the Great) and of almost identical love battles in other Italian operas, as well as being a satirical allusion to the real-life tension between the two sopranos who played these operatic rivals. Of the other characters in *The Beggar's Opera* almost all the men are criminals of one sort or another and almost all the women are whores. Just as Jane Austen's characters in *Northanger Abbey* are antitypes of the stereotyped figures of the Gothic novel as well as self-sufficient novelistic characters, Gay's characters are antitypes of operatic stereotypes as well as self-sufficient dramatic characters. *The Beggar's Opera* is undoubtedly true to its title in that it controverts every normal operatic expectation. The nobility of character, dignity of conduct, and refinement of both sentiment and language characteristic of Italian opera are largely replaced by the attitudes, behaviour and idiom of the underworld.

However, Gay cleverly exploits, for burlesque as well as for other purposes, the discrepancy between operatic expectations and what he provides, especially in his treatment of his "operatic hero" Macheath; thus he ensures that the burlesque level is not lost sight of behind the layers of social and political satire. In some ways Macheath acts and sounds like an operatic hero. The first words he *speaks,* "Suspect my Honour, my Courage, suspect any thing but my Love" (1.13), have a distinctly heroic note, and Polly's reply, with its unquestioning assumption that her highwayman-husband is on a par with Hercules or Alexander the Great, makes the burlesque parallel explicit: "I have no Reason to doubt you, for I find in the Romance you lent me, none of the great Heroes were ever false in Love." Polly's father, even at the moment of arresting Macheath in act 2, scene 5, makes an identical connection between his son-in-law and the sort of men normally presented as operatic heroes: "Your Case, Mr. Macheath, is not particular. The greatest Heroes have been ruin'd by Women." Lucy too acknowledges the "heroic" status of Macheath, as in her first remark on visiting him in the condemned cell: "There is nothing moves one so much as a great Man in Distress" (3.15). In his dealings with his gang, Macheath clearly sees himself as the equivalent of a military leader like Alexander and actually behaves with the magnanimity expected of an operatic hero. He claims to be brave, loyal, fair-minded, and generous: "Is there any man who suspects my Courage? . . . My

Honour and Truth to the Gang? . . . In the Division of our Booty, have I ever shown the least Marks of Avarice or Injustice?" (2.2). And in act 3, scene 4, when two members of his gang are short of money after failing to steal anything, he keeps his word by digging into his own pockets: "I am sorry, Gentlemen, the Road was so barren of Money. When my Friends are in Difficulties, I am always glad that my Fortune can be serviceable to them." Here as elsewhere he addresses members of the gang as "Gentlemen," insisting that they are all honourable: "I have a fixt Confidence, Gentlemen, in you all, as Men of Honour, and as such I value and respect you" (2.2) and "But we, Gentlemen, have still Honour enough to break through the Corruptions of the World" (3.4). In all such passages, the mock-heroic incongruity between the criminals who act, speak, and are spoken about, on the one hand, and the conduct and the sentiments expressed, on the other, registers as ironic burlesque.

Gay's use of familiar melodies, especially simple ballad tunes, as opposed to the elaborate arias of Italian opera is the musical equivalent of his making an operatic hero out of Macheath rather than someone like Alexander. The fact that the criminal characters of *The Beggar's Opera* burst into song in the manner of operatic figures in itself creates burlesque humour; and while it is unlikely that Gay intended to parody any specific arias, he does occasionally enhance the burlesque by making the hackneyed similes mentioned in the introduction by the Beggar express attitudes, especially toward love, which are not found in the relatively chaste world of Italian opera. The simile of "the Moth," for example, appears in air 4, "If Love the Virgin's Heart invade," in which Mrs. Peachum reflects that if her daughter, like any other girl, "plays about the Flame" and loses her virginity, she may end up as a whore—"Her Honour's sing'd, and then for Life, / She's—what I dare not name." Gay also links operatic simile, in this case "the Flower," with the fate of deflowered virgins in Polly's song about her politic motives for retaining her virginity, air 6, "Virgins are like the fair Flower in its Lustre"; this is intended to reassure her father that she knows how to "grant some Things, and refuse what is most material," although she has in fact secretly married Macheath. In each of these songs the operatic simile is burlesqued by being made to convey nonoperatic subject matter, but it is simultaneously rinsed clean in order to express a truth about the realities of contemporary life. The girl who succumbed to her sexual desires premaritally was, like the moth in the flame, quite likely to destroy herself. If she was known to have lost her virginity, she might well be cast out of the society that had nurtured her, and left to her own resources which usually meant prostitution. In Polly's song, Gay clarifies the severity of a social code that demanded such a penalty for a momentary human failing, and also conveys the fragility of virginity and the sense of sadness at its loss, by means of the very image which he is burlesquing. It is Gay's inspired juxtaposition of a natural garden and Covent Garden, which was a redlight district as well as London's vegetable, fruit, and flower market, that makes this possible. The cut flower ("once pluck'd, 'tis no longer alluring") being sent by the gardener to the market at Covent Garden signifies the deflowered virgin being virtually forced by society to the other Covent Garden, the flesh market of the brothels ("There fades, and shrinks, and grows past all enduring, / Rots, stinks, and dies, and is trod under feet").

In other airs the discrepancy between what the simile normally conveys in opera and what it conveys in *The Beggar's Opera* is much less marked or even nonexistent; but because of the incongruity between the conceited linguistic idiom of opera and the unoperatic singer as well as the popular tune, the burlesque effect is still recognizable. Lucy's outburst of distress in air 47, "I'm like a Skiff on the Ocean tost," when she believes that Polly is "sporting on Seas of Delight" with Macheath and decides on a plan of revenge as the only way to appease her jealousy, employs "the Ship" simile mentioned by the Beggar in the introduction; this therefore takes the form of an operatic cliché, for such outbursts of distress and jealousy were fairly common in Italian opera. Other airs, especially Polly's most tender expressions of devoted love for Macheath, also have operatic antecedents. Air 34, "Thus when the Swallow, seeking Prey," is the most obvious case since the Beggar points it out in speaking of the simile of "The Swallow"; but air 13, "The Turtle thus with plaintive crying," which is sung when Polly discovers that her parents are determined to arrange Macheath's execution and which features the conventional comparison of lovers to turtledoves, is very similar. Shortly afterwards, Macheath and Polly are alone together for the first time in the play, and this scene (1.13), in which they declare their love for each other before having to part, contains no less than five airs, including three duets. The marked preponderance of song in itself indicates a parallel to operatic love scenes, and in his fine essay on the play, Bertrand H. Bronson tentatively suggests that Gay may have had in mind a scene between parting lovers in Handel's *Floridante* (1721); one of the duets (air 16) in particular bears some resemblance to the impassioned avowals of everlasting love by Elmira and Floridante.

Bronson argues that several other situations in *The Beggar's Opera* may have specific operatic sources. The way in which Macheath is arrested in a tavern (2.5) could be based on the attempt on Ptolemy's life in a seraglio in Handel's *Giulio Cesare* (1724), and the quarrel between Peachum and Lockit (2.10) possibly owes something to another scene between arguing fathers in Handel's *Flavio* (1723). In the latter case, however, the main source is the quarrel between Brutus and Cassius in Shakespeare's *Julius Caesar* and the similarity to the operatic scene may be no more than a coincidence. Whether Gay intended these very specific situational correspondences remains hypothetical. However, especially in the closing stages of *The Beggar's Opera* there are several unmistakable though general parallels with Italian opera, and these culminate in the coup de théâtre when the two characters from the introduction, the Beggar and the Player, enter to produce a happy ending out of apparent catastrophe.

First of all there is Lucy's attempt to eliminate her rival, Polly, by poisoning her (3.7–10). Having helped Macheath to escape from Newgate, Lucy is tormented by "Jealousy, Rage, Love and Fear" because she believes, wrongly, that he is with Polly. Lucy has "the Rats-bane ready," and when Polly comes to visit her at Newgate, Lucy suggests that they have a drink to cheer themselves up. But at the moment when Lucy forces a glass containing the poison on Polly, the recaptured Macheath is brought back to the prison and Polly is so shaken at the sight of him in chains that she drops the glass and spills its contents. Gay undoubtedly bases this episode on a popular feature of a number of contemporary Italian operas, the scene set in a prison in which one of the principal characters narrowly escapes death in the form of a cup of poison. These incidents take various forms, but in several of Handel's operas produced not long before *The Beggar's Opera,* the hero seems doomed to die by drinking a cup of poison yet is saved as a result of a last-second intervention during which the cup is upset. In *Radamisto* (1720), for example, the heroine Zenobia is forced by Tiridate to take a bowl of poison to her condemned lover, Radamisto himself, who is shackled and awaiting execution; but when she reaches him, she offers to drink it herself and is prevented only by the sudden entrance of Tiridate who knocks the bowl out of her hands. An almost identical scene occurs in *Floridante*. In *Radamisto* and *Floridante,* the gesture is one of heroic self-sacrifice, and the treatment is intensely emotional. In *The Beggar's Opera,* the action is a cunning and unheroic attempt to commit murder under the pretence of friendship, and the treatment verges on the comic. This whole episode has a further burlesque significance in that it resembles the encounters between rival operatic heroines, such as Rossane and Lisaura in *Alesandro,* where they attempt to discuss their relationships with the hero.

The burlesque parallel continues in the scenes following Macheath's return to Newgate. The kind of prison scene in Italian opera that "the Ladies always reckon charmingly pathetick," to use the Beggar's phrase, is the one outlined above in which a woman visits her lover or husband who is awaiting death; the greater his suffering and her grief, the more "charmingly pathetick" the scene would be. Earlier in *The Beggar's Opera* (2.13), Gay provides a counterpart to such scenes by exposing the imprisoned Macheath simultaneously to Polly and Lucy, each of whom regards herself as his wife. The result, a comic confrontation between a rake and two of his women, one of whom, Lucy, is pregnant by him, is the antithesis of the decorous intensity of operatic prison scenes; it also travesties the situation of a hero like Alesandro, who is faced with an almost impossible choice between Rossane and Lisaura. Macheath, under verbal bombardment from both Polly and Lucy, responds in the rollicking and impudent air 35, "How happy could I be with either," by deciding to ignore both of them. The operatic parallel is considerably reinforced by Gay's subsequent use of two duets in this scene. In air 36, "I'm bubbled" ("bubbled" means "deceived"), the vocal line passes back and forth between Polly and Lucy just as it does between the singers of operatic duets, especially rival heroines; but the situation from which the song arises, their discovery of Macheath's duplicity in making identical promises to both of them, is unlike anything to be found in Italian opera. Air 38, "Why how now, Madam Flirt?" in which Polly and Lucy attack each other verbally, differs in that the vocal line does not alternate throughout; instead Lucy sings the first stanza and Polly the second. Of particular interest here is the fact that the monosyllabic words at the end of the third line of each stanza, "Dirt" and "made," must be sung in melismatic or coloratura style, each word running for seventeen notes and occupying almost three bars. Such ornate, bravura singing is standard in operatic arias but very rare in folk songs and ballads, and is the only sustained example in *The Beggar's Opera,* where Gay usually fits one syllable to one note of music. That Gay should draw such attention to the operatic parallel in this song is doubly significant since nowhere else is the rivalry between Polly and Lucy so bitterly and vulgarly expressed. The contrast between matter and operatic manner is therefore exceptionally pronounced, and this in turn highlights the undignified personal behaviour of Francesca Cuzzoni and Faustina Bordoni in comparison with the dignified roles they took in operas. Offstage the prima donnas behaved as Polly and Lucy do onstage.

In the closing scenes Gay again brings Polly, Lucy, and Macheath together in Newgate after Lucy's attempt to poison Polly (3.11). This encounter between the highwayman and his two "wives" is less obviously a travesty of "charmingly pathetick" prison scenes, but the continuing competition between the women for Macheath's attention, especially when it takes the form of a duet in air 52, "Hither, dear Husband, turn your Eyes," sustains the operatic burlesque. The way in which one voice takes over from the other like an echo in the second half of the song (" 'Tis Polly sues. / 'Tis Lucy speaks") imitates a feature of many operatic duets. As before, Macheath's predicament as expressed in air 53, "Which way shall I turn me?—How can I decide?" is the essentially comic one of a philanderer, who is expert at handling one woman at a time, becoming helpless and retreating into silence when face-to-face with two of his conquests; again it alludes to the dilemma confronting Alessandro and some other heroes. If John O. Rees is correct in interpreting this scene as a mock-heroic version of the classical myth called The Judgment (or Choice) of Hercules, the burlesque resemblance to opera is greatly enhanced since Hercules was a very suitable candidate for operatic treatment. In the myth, Hercules is confronted by two goddesses, Virtue and Pleasure (or Vice), and has to decide between them. This subject was popular with creative artists from the Renaissance onwards because it allowed them to present a metaphysical and moral conflict as a dramatic and concretely realized situation; in the eighteenth century it was treated by several poets and composers in England, including

Handel. The symmetrical arrangement of Gay's characters, with Polly and her father on one side of Macheath, and Lucy and her father on the other, is very similar to the usual formal organization of painted versions of the myth and could well be modelled on them; but it would be wrong to push the parallel too far by identifying Polly with Virtue and Lucy with Pleasure.

As an interlude before the scene changes to the condemned cell, Gay specifies "A Dance of Prisoners in Chains" at the end of act 3, scene 12. This plainly grotesque dance is a low-life counterpart to the dignified ballet dancing that had been incorporated in many operas since the seventeenth century, and the completely arbitrary way in which it is introduced is itself a comment on the frequent insertion of dances into operas with little or no dramatic justification. The burlesque intention is much more obvious here than in the "Dance a la ronde in the French Manner" in act 2, scene 4, but although this may sound more formal and operatic, it is not performed by deities in a temple or by aristocrats in a court but by Macheath and eight whores in a tavern near Newgate. It too is introduced in a gratuitous way when Macheath hears harp music: "But hark! I hear musick. . . . E'er you seat your selves, Ladies, what think you of a Dance?"

When the scene does change to the condemned cell (3.13), Macheath sings a soliloquy to music taken from no less than ten different songs so that the ten airs 58–67 coalesce into an extended piece of singing. Nowhere else in the play does Gay use fragments of tunes and nowhere else does one air follow another without any speech intervening. Of the ten airs, one consists of one line, six consist of two lines, two consist of four lines, and only the final one of eight lines is of average length. Despite the Beggar's initial claim that his opera contains "no Recitative," Macheath's segmented utterance and abrupt changes of tune, interrupted only when he pours himself stiff drinks, is not unlike operatic recitative, especially as it concludes with a full-length air in the same way as recitative prepares the way for an aria. In opera such rapid changes of thought and emotion as Macheath's can be encompassed only in recitative, never in arias. From Gay's scrupulous avoidance before this of anything resembling recitative, one would expect the bulk of Macheath's monologue to be spoken; so the startling use of song is extremely effective in bringing home the operatic parallel. At the level of burlesque, Macheath's "recitative and aria" is a mockery of those sung by operatic heroes in prison. Instead of exhibiting courage and fortitude while awaiting execution, like Floridante in Handel's opera who even welcomes death as a deliverance, the much more human Macheath drinks heavily in a not very successful attempt to go to the gallows bravely and concentrates his thoughts on alcohol and women.

The one sung trio, air 68, "Would I might be hang'd!" occurs at what might be called the most "charmingly pathetick" moment when Polly and Lucy visit Macheath in the condemned cell just before he is about to be taken to Tyburn to be hanged (3.15). Since these three characters are on stage together in a number of scenes, there are several opportunities for trios; Polly and Lucy actually sing duets in front of Macheath, but only here do all three share an air. Gay is again following operatic precedent, because it is common in opera for the principal characters (if there are three) to join in a trio at the climax of the work. The cowardly but credible behaviour of Macheath, who has run out of alcohol ("I tremble! I droop!—See, my Courage is out"), is the antithesis of, for example, Floridante's operatic heroics in the face of death, and the yearning of both Polly and Lucy to share Macheath's fate on the gallows ("Would I might be hang'd! / And I would so too!") is a comic transformation of the attempts by self-sacrificing operatic heroines to kill themselves in order to save their lovers' lives. Gay's choice of tune for this "Hanging Trio" could hardly have been better since "All you that must take a Leap" was a ballad about the execution of two criminals. The burlesque effect is greatly intensified at this point by the sudden arrival of four more of Macheath's "wives," each accompanied by a child, so that he is confronted by no less than six of his "wives" and four of his children. Gay deliberately plunges what in opera would be intended to be a profoundly moving climax to the level of farce. Ironically, only in this ludicrous situation does Macheath acquire the moral strength of an operatic hero and welcome death as a deliverance: "What—four Wives more!—This is too much.—Here—tell the Sheriffs Officers I am ready." The travesty of opera could hardly be taken further, yet Gay does just that in the next scene.

As Macheath is led away, the action is interrupted and the dramatic illusion shattered by the entry of the Player and the Beggar (3.16). This is a low-life equivalent of the device known as the deus ex machina, common in heroic drama, tragicomedy and opera after

the Restoration, and involving a surprise intervention or unex-
pected discovery that produces a virtually magical transformation at
a stroke. No matter how closely Italian operas approached tragedy,
happy endings were de rigeur, and the contrived denouements ne-
cessitated by this convention were particularly vulnerable to hostile
criticism. At the end of *Arsinoe,* for example, Dorisbe stabs herself
melodramatically after being rejected in love, but in no time at all
she participates in the finale, explaining that her wound is not serious. In opera after opera the villain redeems himself at the end of
the third act, and however diabolically he has behaved throughout,
he suddenly becomes penitent and is reconciled with the other characters. In *The Beggar's Opera* the Player prevents the law taking its
natural course by expostulating to the Beggar about Macheath's im-
minent execution. To the Player's surprise, the Beggar admits that
he is "for doing strict poetical Justice" with Macheath executed and
all the other characters hanged or transported. But he gives way in
the face of the Player's irrefutable argument:

> PLAYER: Why then, Friend, this is a down-right deep
> Tragedy. The Catastrophe is manifestly wrong, for
> an Opera must end happily.
> BEGGAR: Your Objection, Sir, is very just; and is easily
> remov'd. For you must allow, that in this kind of
> Drama, 'tis no matter how absurdly things are
> brought about.—So—you Rabble there—run and
> cry a Reprieve—let the Prisoner be brought back to
> his Wives in Triumph.
> PLAYER: All this we must do, to comply with the Taste
> of the Town.

The play can then end with a song and a dance to celebrate Macheath's release. What is so ingenious about this episode is that it allows Gay to criticize explicitly Italian opera and its fans, to
burlesque by means of Macheath's reprieve the miraculous reversals
of fortune and character with which operas frequently end, and at
the same time to secure a fitting conclusion to what is, after all, a
comedy. *The Beggar's Opera* demands a nontragic ending, and in
rescuing Macheath, Gay makes a virtue of necessity—indeed, several virtues. There is even a political innuendo in Macheath's unex-
pected escape from death; during the difficult situation following
George I's death in 1727, Sir Robert Walpole surprisingly avoided

political extinction by promising the new king, George II, more money for the royal family. The burlesque is given an added pungency by the completely arbitrary nature of Macheath's reprieve, which is in no way earned and is not accompanied by any moral transformation. His promise of fidelity to Polly, "I take Polly for mine . . . And for Life, you Slut,—for we were really marry'd" (3.17), cannot be taken too seriously considering the value of his earlier promises, not to mention his condescending though admittedly affectionate use of "Slut."

Today, Gay's burlesque of Italian opera seems much less significant than his social satire, which is more immediately accessible to us, and criticism of the play understandably concentrates on such literary qualities as irony and imagery. Nevertheless, Gay aimed to create an original type of opera by turning the conventions of Italian opera upside down so that he was simultaneously poking fun at them, and this attempt lies behind the overall structure of *The Beggar's Opera* and the detailed organization of many of its parts. The continuing popularity of the work means that it is possible to enjoy it without being aware that it burlesques Italian opera, just as it is possible to enjoy *Northanger Abbey* without knowing anything about the Gothic novel; but the subtlety and skill of Gay's design cannot be fully appreciated without grasping the extent to which he uses, *mutatis mutandis,* stock operatic features and situations. *The Beggar's Opera* is much more than a mock-opera, but at one level that is what it is. In addition, it is ultimately impossible to separate the social satire from the operatic burlesque since they are two sides of the same coin. . . . To the literary critic, Gay's use of language is so absorbing that it is easy to forget that he wrote the play for the theatre and for part-musical performance. But the main reason that *The Beggar's Opera* appealed so much to theatregoers in 1728 and has held the stage ever since is not that it is a literary masterpiece, but that it is a lively and unconventional musical comedy, a kind of opera.

Beggars and Thieves

Michael Denning

The Beggar's Opera is too familiar a play. We know it before we read it, in part because of the Brecht/Weill adaptation. Popular songs have made Macheath and Polly Peachum well-known figures. But even when we read *The Beggar's Opera* it seems familiar; the device of comparing statesmen to criminals is a contemporary device; and given the fortunes of the word "impeach," we have little difficulty substituting Nixon for Walpole. Francis Ford Coppola's *The Godfather* is a recent version of the rich figure of organized crime. Literary critics aid in this familiarization; to take one example, William Empson reads the *Opera* as a protoromantic work, embodying the "cult of independence," and forshadowing the modern romanticization of criminals: he compares Macheath to a Chicago tough (of the 1920s and 1930s).

Given this familiarity, I think it is important to insist on the historicity of the work, a play of the English 1720s, and to see it as a condensation, a figuration, of contradictions within that society. To restore to this drama its role in providing an imagination of difference in our supermarket culture is the aim of this essay. But to avoid writing the history of the past in terms of the present is difficult.

The obvious place to begin in situating the work would be to uncover what is being satirized, that which is not on the surface of the play, to pull Walpole and the fashion of the Italian opera out

From *Literature and History* 8, no. 1 (Spring 1982). © 1982 by the Thames Polytechnic, London.

from historical oblivion. But I would like to begin at the familiar surface, not with the object of satire but with the vehicle by which it is satirized: Gay's choice of thieves and highwaymen. It seems a natural device to us; perhaps we need to estrange it. Frank Chandler, in his comprehensive history of rogue literature, tells us that satire enters the English literature of roguery with Gay and Fielding. And E. P. Thompson writes that "it was in these years that the comparison of statesmanship with criminality became common coinage" (*Whigs and Hunters*). On the other hand, we know that Walpole was satirized in other ways: as a philistine who could not recognize true poetry; and as a quack doctor unable to cure a sick nation. The choice of the criminal is something new in the 1720s. In this essay I will begin with a look at the figure of Jonathan Wild, the basis for both Gay and Fielding's satires; will then look at the institution of hanging; and finally will consider the struggles over the law in the early eighteenth century. My three main anchors are: Empson's essay on the *Opera;* the work of the Warwick Centre for Social History; and the work of Michel Foucault on punishment.

THE IDEOLOGY OF THE GANG

We can take an odd misreading of *The Beggar's Opera* as a place to begin. Gerald Howson, author of the definitive biography of Jonathan Wild, writes that after his death "Jonathan Wild had become a symbol rather than a remembered historical person. . . . In *The Beggar's Opera,* John Gay had tried to show that 'Peachum' and 'Lockit' . . . were really pillars of the underworld; but his point was missed, for politicians saw the play only as an attack on themselves, and critics attacked the play because it showed criminals in a humorous and sympathetic light" (*Thief-Taker General*). It is difficult to see how the *Opera* could be taken as an exposé of the underworld in the manner of a "true-to-life" Mafia paperback; one thinks the politicians and critics have seen at least something of the play. But the vehicle of the play is the underworld and the popular figure of Jonathan Wild, so it is worthwhile to investigate this a little more. Jonathan Wild was, Howson tells us, "the subject of more 'Accounts,' 'Narratives' and 'Lives' than any other criminal of the 18th century." So we are involved in a double displacement, requiring two explanations: why is Wild so central to the popular imagination, and is he a representative figure? And, how does Gay transform the myth of Wild, and what does that transformation mean?

What is the character of crime in the 1720s? J. M. Beattie, in an account of crime in England from 1660 to 1800, quotes a pamphlet written against Wild which speaks of "the general complaint of the taverns, the coffeehouses, the shop-keepers and others, that their customers are afraid when it is dark to come to their houses and shops for fear . . . that they may be blinded, knocked down, cut or stabbed." Beattie adds that "such comments can be found at other times, of course, but there seems to be a particular concentration of concern in the 1720s in newspapers, in the correspondence of those engaged in judicial administration, and in the masses of contemporary accounts of crime, including, in Defoe's novels, the first fictional accounts of criminal life" ("The Pattern of Crime in England: 1660–1800," *Past and Present* 62 [1974]). E. P. Thompson has written that "if that unsatisfactory term 'crime wave' could ever be used with conviction, it might possibly be applied to the early 1720s." However, to add one more authority, Douglas Hay writes that "it appears as if it is not just a matter of 'crime' enlarging but equally of a property-conscious oligarchy redefining, through its legislative power, activities, use-rights in common or woods, perquisites in industry, as thefts and offences" (*Albion's Fatal Tree*). It was a time when capital punishment was being extended to more and more crimes, crimes not between people but against property. The Black Act of 1723 added some fifty offences, mostly poaching rabbits and fish and hunting deer, to the death penalty. Locke had written that "government has no other end but the preservation of property," and the Whig government was pursuing that end with a vengeance. This, together with the suspension of habeas corpus because of the revelations of Jacobite conspiracies in 1722, and the financial disorder following the South Sea Bubble in 1720 (in which Gay lost money), led to a repressive state in the 1720s (which Whig historians term "the establishment of political stability"). It is against this background that the career and celebrity of Jonathan Wild is to be seen.

Wild was not a highwayman or thief. He maintained himself as a respectable Londoner working as a thief-taker and a restorer of lost property. As thief-taker, he captured criminals and brought them to prison, collecting the rewards. As a restorer of lost property, he maintained offices in the Old Bailey and enabled people who had had property stolen to retrieve it. He had agents throughout southern England. In the process he destroyed four London gangs; the Privy Council consulted him over ways to combat crime. These activities were welcomed and applauded by the community; Wild even petitioned to become a Freeman of London, and thereby to gain a sort of official recognition for his position. Since there was no regular police force, the thief-taking system was, Howson tells us, "the most effective and least expensive way of keeping crime under control." The revelations, after his fall, that Wild, far from preventing crime, was the organizer of the largest crime network in London, were shocking. The thief-taking had been a means of establishing his reputation and controlling his subordinates; at his trial he published a list of those petty criminals he had sent to the gallows. The lost property office had not only arranged the return of property but had planned the robbery of it.

A number of pamphlets were written on Wild, narrating his life and system; I want to look briefly at the one written by Daniel Defoe shortly after Wild's execution in 1725. Defoe, who claims to have gone to Wild's Lost Property Office to inquire about a sword he had had stolen, emphasizes the "business" side of Wild:

> He openly kept his Compting House, or Office, like a Man of Business, and had his Books to enter every thing in with the utmost Exactness and Regularity . . . he took none of your Money for restoring your Goods neither did he restore you any Goods; you gave him Money indeed for his Trouble in enquiring out the Thief, and for using his Interest by awing or perswading to get your stolen Goods sent you back, telling you what you must give to the Porter that brings them, if you please, for he does not oblige you to give it.

But Defoe's disbelief is not directed to Wild but to his society, including himself, for tolerating, even applauding, what could not have been that surprising:

> He was now Master of his Trade, Poor and Rich flock'd to him: If any thing was Lost, (whether by Negligence in the Owner, or Vigilance and Dexterity in the Thief) away we went to Jonathan Wild. Nay, Advertisements were Publish'd, directing the Finder of almost every Thing, to bring it to Jonathan Wild, who was eminently impower'd to take it, and give the Reward. How Infatu-

ate were the People of this Nation all the while? Did they consider, that at the very time that they treated this Person with such a Confidence, as if he had been appointed to the Trade? He had, perhaps, the very Goods in his keeping, waiting the Advertisement for the Reward; and that, perhaps, they had been stolen with that very Intention?

Defoe also points out that the crowd at Tyburn, contrary to their usual compassion for the condemned, hurled "curses and execrations" at Wild, and that there was "not one pitying Eye to be seen." This is in marked contrast to the hero of another of Defoe's criminal biographies, Jack Sheppard. Sheppard was a thief who was betrayed by Wild and then gained fame and sympathy by a series of extraordinary escapes, which Defoe narrates. His small size and Cockney wit made him the antithesis of Wild in the popular imagination, the boy who was first seduced to crime by, depending on the story, either a woman, Edgworth Bess, or Wild himself, and was betrayed by the two together. Defoe has Sheppard denounce thief-takers and the practice of impeaching; it hurts the "Reputation of the British Thievery." Empson is wrong when he says Gay split Wild into Peachum and Macheath, into villain and hero. Rather, Gay used the popular opposition of Wild and Sheppard; when Fielding fuses Sheppard and Wild in his character of Jonathan Wild, the meaning, as we shall see, slips again.

The most important aspect of Defoe's Wild pamphlet is its rejection of satire. Attacking the comic and satiric versions of Wild's life, he says

The following Tract does not indeed make a Jest of his Story as they do, or present his History, which indeed is a tragedy of itself, in the stile of Mockery and Redicule, but in a Method agreeable to the Fact. They that had rather have a Falsehood to laugh at, than a true Account of Things to inform them, had best buy the Fiction, and leave the History to those who know how to distinguish Good from Evil.

Defoe maintains this moral tone a few years later when he comments on the portrayal of rogues: "We take pains to puff 'em up in their villainy, and thieves are set out in so amiable a light in *The Beggar's Opera* that it has taught them to value themselves on their profession, rather than to be asham'd of it."

But satire held sway; its ambivalence may be seen in that it begins with Wild's own pamphlet, *An Answer to a Late Insolent Libel,* published in 1718, satirizing the attack on thief-takers made by Charles Hitchens in an earlier pamphlet. Wild replies to a basically accurate account of his own illegal activities with ridicule and innuendo, and indeed wins the paper war, going on to consolidate his organization. After Wild's execution, there were satiric lives and an *Advice to His Successors.* But more serious satire arose by the coincidence of the exposure and execution of Wild and the impeachment of the Earl of Macclesfield, the Lord Chancellor, for bribery in 1725. The opposition journalist Nathaniel Mist first elaborated the Wild-Walpole analogy in 1725, and Swift is supposed (though I don't see any evidence of it) to have first dubbed Wild "The Great."

Before going on to Gay's satire, the question remains: was Jonathan Wild a representative figure, and what does his infamy signify? E. P. Thompson, in his study of the Black Act, deals with the question of whether the Blacks were a "gang"; he says that the category of "gang" or the twentieth-century criminological term, "subculture," can be applied to some criminal activity in London, like that around Wild, which was professionalised and institutionalized; but that "in the eighteenth century it is probable that only a fraction of those who were caught up in the law—or who were hanged and transported—belonged to this professionalized sector." "What is at issue," he goes on to say,

> is not whether there were any such gangs (there were) but the universality with which the authorities applied the term to any association of people, from a benefit society to a group of kin to a Fagin's den which fell outside the law. This was partly self-delusion in the minds of the magistracy, and unwillingness to acknowledge the extent of disaffection with which they were faced . . . it was somehow comforting to assert that these outrages were the work of a gang.

And though Thompson does not mention it, it may be significant that in 1726 an act was passed prohibiting combinations of workers. That neither the Waltham Blacks nor King John, a Robin Hood figure, had any such celebrity as Wild leads to the conclusion that the accounts of Wild, whether realistic or romantic, whether fictions or histories, are less representations of England in the 1720s, even of the underworld, than embodiments of a powerful ideology of the "gang"—seeing ideology not as a system of ideas or a false consciousness, but as a sort of narrative which creates an imaginary relationship for the individual to the collective world. Gay, by taking up the Wild story, stages not the "cult of independence" but this ideology of the gang.

How does Gay structure his version of Jonathan Wild? The basic opposition among the characters is that between Macheath and Peachum. There are a number of semantic contraries by which we can express this: youth/age, prodigality/miserliness, escape/imprisonment, aristocrat/bourgeois, eros/money. To take the last contrary, we see this clearly made when Macheath's review of the "ladies" (2.4) parallels Peachum's earlier review of his gang (1.3). But it is a mark of the interdependence of the contraries that the characters define their own passion in the terms of their opposites. So Macheath says that "money is not so strong a cordial" as women (2.3), compares his parting with Polly to the parting of a miser and a shilling (1.13), and says that "a man who loves money might as well be contented with one guinea, as I with one woman" (2.3). For Peachum and Lockit, on the other hand, love, sex and marriage are forms of money: "a handsome wench in our way of business is as profitable as at the bar of a Temple coffee-house" (1.4); Mrs. Peachum says "I am very sensible, husband, that Captain Macheath is worth money" (1.9); the estate of widowhood is seen as the intention of all marriage articles; and Lockit says to Lucy of Macheath's escape: "Perhaps you have made a better bargain with him than I could have done—How much, my good girl?" (3.1). The interdependence of contraries is also evident in the inverted opposition between Polly/Lucy and Jenny Diver (like Peachum and Lockit, Polly and Lucy are identical; Lucy is more accurate than she intends when she says "Then our cases, my dear Polly, are exactly alike. Both of us indeed have been too fond" [3.8]). Whereas Polly and Lucy are shopkeepers' daughters who in part reject their mercenary education for the romance of love and the imitation of the gentry, Jenny is the one of the "'fine ladies" who is thoroughly on Peachum's side: it is said of her that she acts "as if money were her only pleasure. Now that is a command of the passions uncommon in a woman" (2.4). And she has a bourgeois scorn for the gaming table: "cards and dice are only fit for cowardly cheats."

This economy of contraries is attenuated by certain categories that encompass both contraries, and by an imbalance of power between the contraries. In the first case, it is clear that though there are two types of rogues, all are rogues; that though there are two types of predators, all are predators; and that whatever their pleasure, sex and money are not far apart in all minds. In the second case, there is a clear inequality of power between Macheath and Peachum. Lockit and Peachum, being good accountants, know their mutual interest; Peachum says "for you know we have it in our power to hang each other" (2.10). For Macheath that knowledge is the product of the education of the play. Early in the play he says that "business cannot go on without" Peachum, that he is a "necessary agent," and that "the moment we break loose from him, our gang is ruin'd" (2.2). But by the end, in what Empson sees as the only straight line in the play, Macheath says of Peachum and Lockit: "their lives are as much in your power, as yours are in theirs. . . . Tis my last request—Bring those villains to the gallows before you, and I am satisfied" (3.14). But one is not really convinced; Gay cannot hang his villain.

The detailing of these oppositions is little more than descriptive. But if meaning is created by difference, something may be gained by seeing how they differ from another telling of the Wild tale. So I will turn briefly to Henry Fielding's novel of 1743, *Jonathan Wild*.

First of all, Fielding's Wild is, as I have said earlier, a mixture of the figures of Wild and Jack Sheppard, or in other words, of Peachum and Macheath. Fielding's Wild is a thief-taker, he employs other hands to steal for him and impeaches them when it is profitable. He has a gang which we are told is regularized and organized; there is a brief account of the office for the return of stolen goods. But one feels that these are used because they are given in the life of the real Wild; they are not the sources of the narrative energy. Indeed the novel plays down the organized gang and the business aspects of Wild. When Fielding's Wild divides mankind into "those that use their own hands, and those who employ the hands of others," he undercuts this by dividing the second group into "those who employ hands for the use of the community in which they live" (by whom he means "the yeoman, the manufacturer, the merchant, and perhaps the gentlemen"), and "those who employ hands merely for their own use" (he lists conquerors, statesmen, and thieves). Fielding's Wild is not a shopkeeper; he is closer to rogue than thief-taker, courting and abducting women, picking pockets, aiding and encouraging escapes from justice, gambling at cards and dice; he is an aristocratic man of fashion, a beau. So the aspects of Gay's villain are played down, and those of Gay's hero become villainous. This is emphasized in that whereas Gay's victims are themselves rogues, Fielding's victims are innocent. The Heartfrees and their apprentice, Friendly, are good-natured and generous; their peaceful existence is destroyed by the intrusion of Wild. They are the good bourgeois family that Peachum's family parodies: at the end the faithful apprentice marries the daughter and becomes a partner in the successful business. Placed on the grid of the *Opera,* this would be something like Filch marrying Polly.

Fielding's novel turns the contradictions of the Wild story as written by Gay into a bourgeois morality play much like the original criminal pamphlets. We are given the vicarious thrill in the life of the aristocratic villain (since the Heartfrees are neither very exciting nor very convincing) and are then gratified to see the villain brought to justice (Fielding's Wild, like the real Wild but unlike Gay's Peachum, is hanged). That this is, despite its satire on Walpole (who was no longer in power when this was published in 1743; there is evidence that Fielding suppressed the novel in return for money earlier), a Whiggish tale is seen by the dominant oppositions of liberty/tyranny and law/lawlessness, neither of which are to be found in Gay. This is also, I think, a real expression of the "cult of independence," not by glorifying the criminal, as the romantics were to do, but by exploring the paradoxes and dangers of the new individualism.

To return to *The Beggar's Opera:* in the staging of the ideology of the gang, the moral problem of the play becomes a political one. For the gang is not just a party, a conspiracy, a set of evil individuals; it is the new system, the mercantile commercial capitalism. E. P. Thompson writes that "Political life in England in the 1720s had something of the sick quality of a 'banana republic.' This is a recognized phase of commercial capitalism when predators fight for the spoils of power and have not yet agreed to submit to rational or bureaucratic rules and forms. Each politician, by nepotism, interest and purchase, gathered around him a following of loyal dependents." Gay senses the power of this system; this is why his heroes are not outside it. Macheath is part of the gang; the aristocracy and court are no longer an alternative to the money of the City but a parasite on it. They are all part of a system where "money is the true fuller's earth for reputation" (1.9). Money has no origin, no smell; it doesn't distinguish between a thief, a shopkeeper or a gentleman. And this is why Gay cannot hang Peachum. No one has that power except Lockit, and these two are beginning to evolve rational and bureaucratic rules between themselves. But just choosing thieves as heroes and making businessmen thieves is a challenge to the contemporary deification of property. When Mrs. Peachum says to her husband, "You know, my dear, I never meddle in matters of death," it is clear that death and business are one for Gay.

How does Gay come to do this? Surely not in the way of this essay, from a reflection of the meaning of contemporary myths of criminality. We can agree with Empson when he says "nor does any one in the discussions about its morality seem to have taken it as against the appalling penal code and prison system." It may be that Gay's own financial losses in the South Sea Bubble turned him against the merchant capitalism of his day; and it may simply be the revenge of a disappointed office-seeker. But I think it may well have been derived from a reflection on the position of the writer in the early eighteenth century: a beggar dependent on the patronage of a government which under Walpole veered away from previous support of men of letters (of all parties). Without that, he had to turn, like Macheath, to the taste of the town.

THE THEATRE OF TYBURN

One critic (Spacks) has written of the play's "particular double view of the world as both horrifying and ridiculous" and of "the general lightheartedness of the play as a whole, lightheartedness which persists, paradoxically, despite the bitterness, the intense cynicism reiterated by the ending." And surely the difficulty with the first part of this essay is that, by concentrating on Macheath's last request to his gang to bring Peachum to the gallows, it misses the lightheartedness of the play, which is clearly the dominant tone. Can a historical reading of The Beggar's Opera give any account of this lightheartedness?

One could begin with the comic form of the play which generates much of its lightheartedness, subsuming somewhat its satiric qualities. But I will begin with hanging, ostensibly one of the more horrifying aspects of the eighteenth century. Peter Linebaugh writes of hanging: "Indeed so often is it, as a symbol of all that is bestial, violent and brutal in 18th-century society, counterposed to the architecture, taste, music and literature of genteel civilization that is has lost whatever accurate connotations it once may have had and has now entered the ranks of the historical cliché" [in *Albion's Fatal Tree,* by Linebaugh, Hay, et al.].

Empson rightly latches on to the plays on the word "hanging," seeing it as a "covert metaphor for true love." But the uses of hanging seem to add to the comedy as well. Despite the battle over the hanging of Macheath, hanging is usually seen as preferable to the given state of things. Obviously Peachum and Lockit want Macheath hanged, and he wants them hanged. But, in addition, Mrs. Peachum had rather seen Polly hanged than married (1.8); the parents (Peachum and Lockit) feel that widowhood by hanging is a desirable state (1.10); and Polly's duty to her parents obliges her to hang Macheath (1.10). Macheath would rather be hanged than suffer the furies of the whores (2.3), and rather than be faced with six wives (3.15). Lucy is willing to be hanged for revenge on Polly (3.7), and would rather see Macheath hanged than in the arms of another (2.15). Both Polly and Lucy would like to see Macheath hanged for revenge at one point (2.13); at another point they would both be hanged with him (3.15). The beggar would like to hang the whole cast. Surely some of the lightheartedness of the play comes from this universal desire to "be hanged."

This lightheartedness about hanging is rooted in the poetry of popular speech. Looking at the slang and the canting dictionaries that record the speech of the eighteenth-century London poor, Peter Linebaugh concludes that "the speech of the labouring class described the hanging with irreverence, humour, and defiance." He then catalogues the metaphors for hanging; I'll quote a few. "To hang, like a dance, was 'to swing,' to 'dance the Paddington frisk,' 'to morris.' It was 'to go west,' 'to ride up Holborn Hill,' to 'dangle in the Sheriff's picture frame,' 'to cry cockles' . . . Awe, majesty and dread were riddled to their proper meaning, death by hanging."

One of the most powerful conceits in the play juxtaposes hangings and weddings. When Macheath says to Polly, "whenever you are talking of marriage, I am thinking of hanging" (2.13), it recalls Polly's early romantic vision of Macheath in the cart being brought to the gallows (1.12). Indeed the play itself, all about hanging, is written, the beggar says, to celebrate a wedding. Empson speaks of the song where the marriage knot and the hangman's knot are linked as the play's "metaphysical poetry." But this is less a strikingly original conceit than a reworking of the hanging custom of the "gallows wedding." Linebaugh, in his account of hanging customs and superstitions, documents the connection between hangings and weddings in speech: "to be 'noozed' in canting talk meant either to be hanged or to be married"; in journalistic simile Defoe is quoted as writing that criminals "go to [their] execution as neat and trim as if they were going to a wedding." He comments also on the actual marriage-like practices at hangings.

One conclusion to be drawn from this historicizing of Gay's figures is that a more adequate object of study for the critic of narrative and figurative language is what Foucault would call a "discursive formation," the general economy of a body of discourses, not in terms of *Zeitgeist* (not to reinstitute a history of ideas) but in terms of its characteristic tropes, figures, and narrative structures, treating that formation to a certain degree anonymously. Without attempting that here, one might use it to situate Gay's poetic practice within that field, if only sketchily. Gay, for example, does not use the canting vocabulary used by Grub Street productions; his position within the genteel literary system prevents that. But the figure of the gallows wedding and the irreverent, lighthearted uses of hanging are central to the play and to its subsequent popularity. One begins to glimpse the contradictions in the play: on the one hand an aristocratic debunking of the middle-class, moralizing sentimental comedy (the Italian opera may have been the direct target because it heightened the artificiality of sentimental comedy—they reign together); on the other hand in its ballads and its rhetoric a play not only "about" the people, but "by" the people.

Hanging creates the comedy of the play not only through its use as word or figure but through its nature as spectacle. The passage where Polly envisions Macheath in the cart to Tyburn strikes us as a bit macabre; but we have not seen such a spectacle; the processions from Newgate to Tyburn were abolished in 1783. Michel Foucault has argued that this was not a quantitative development of less cruelty and more humanity in punishment; it is a qualitative rupture between two very different notions of punishment. He says that "we must rid ourselves of the illusion that penalty is above all a means of reducing crime" (*Discipline and Punish,* translated by A. Sheridan). It is rather a symbolic action with political, religious, and ideological connotations.

The end of the procession, of the public execution, of judicial torture, was the end of punishment regarded as a spectacle. In Gay's time, executions were theatrical events: work stopped, thieves worked, taverns were full. It was a public death. Foucault writes of "the insatiable curiosity that drove spectators to the scaffold to witness the spectacle of sufferings truly endured; there one could decipher crime and innocence, the past and the future, the here below and the eternal." In this performance the main character, Foucault says, was the people. "The people claimed the right to observe the execution and to see who was being executed." And the atmosphere around the execution was often one of a carnival. The hanging day was announced by the ringing of church bells; hawkers sold the broadside ballads, the criminal biographies like those Defoe wrote, and the pamphlets of the last speech of the condemned; people paid to see the condemned in his cell; the procession to Tyburn was along the most heavily travelled roads in London. A contemporary observer wrote: "no solemn procession, it was just the contrary; it was a low-lived black-guard merry-making." In England, unlike the France Foucault writes about, trials were also public, and Howson says that "as far as the Old Bailey was concerned, 'theatre' is less a metaphor than a literal description." The rituals of court, the trumpets and the guards, the sermons and sentences pronounced by the judge, combined to make it a spectacle that people came from all around to witness. As E. P. Thompson writes: "The hegemony of the eighteenth-century gentry and aristocracy was expressed, above all, not in military force, not in the mystifications of a priesthood or the press, not even in economic coercion, but in the rituals in the study of the Justices of the Peace, in the quarter-sessions, in the pomp of Assizes and in the theatre of Tyburn."

The analogy between the theatre and the gallows, particularly in its carnival aspect, may help account for the incongruity that a play so largely about hanging could be so comic. But there is one place where the connection is taken as more than a metaphor: about 1700, "it was remarked that the last time a party had torn down the stage in the city it had set up a scaffold in the court." And if anything seems more foreign to a modern sensibility than the spectacle of hanging, it is the moral attack on the stage. How do we under-

stand the attacks by Jeremy Collier? Can we suspend our own sentiments and see them not as "irrational" or "puritan" absurdities, but
as the coding of a political struggle over a social institution, to be
compared with, for example, the "moral" attacks on modernism of
a Lukacs or a Winters. For it is the same Hanoverian Whigs who
established the ascendency of the gallows, who, with moral arguments (but, more blatantly, political purposes), established the Licensing Act of 1737 in order to control the theatre more closely.
Indeed *The Beggar's Opera,* which mocks the majesty of the gallows, was attacked on moral, not political, grounds. And the performance of Gay's sequel *Polly* was suppressed.

It was also from the reforming wing of the Whigs that the
move to take the spectacle (but not the hanging) out of hanging
arose in the eighteenth century. Foucault writes that "it was evident
that the great spectacle of punishment ran the risk of being rejected
by the very people to whom it was addressed . . . the reformers of
the eighteenth and nineteenth centuries were not to forget that, in
the last resort, the executions did not, in fact, frighten the people."
Indeed there were cases of the crowd rejecting the sentence and saving the condemned, and of riots occurring on execution day. To
conclude I will note that both Defoe and Fielding wanted to end
aspects of the hanging spectacle, with Fielding using a significant
image: "a Murder behind the Scenes, if the Poet knows how to
manage it, will effect the Audience with greater Terror than if it
was acted before their Eyes." Is Gay's spectacle a defence not only
of the stage but of the spectacle of hanging?

Justice: Poetical and . . .

To return to some early questions: why is this "cult of crime
and roguery" so important? Why is this spectacle of the scaffold so
important? How does Gay produce (in the sense of producing a
play) these figures? Why is *The Beggar's Opera* the most performed
piece of the eighteenth century?

Douglas Hay gives us part of the answer: "the ideology of the
ruling oligarchy, which places a supreme value upon property,
finds its visible and material embodiment above all in the ideology
and practice of the law. Tyburn Tree, as William Blake well understood, stood at the heart of this ideology; and its ceremonies were
at the heart of the popular culture also." I have looked at the ideol-

ogy of the gang and at the treatment of hanging in Gay, both of which are part of this ideology of the law. I have suggested that certain contradictions fissure the play; I have not yet shown that. In this final section, I will look at the escapes in the play, so as to return to two of Empson's points in order to make more explicit Gay's contradictory production of this ideology. Empson's points are: first, his claim that "the essential process behind the *Opera* [is] a resolution of heroic and pastoral into a cult of independence"; and second, his claim that the *Opera* is an "art-form that not merely evades but breaks through [the class system], that makes the classes feel part of a larger unity or simply at home with each other."

There are three escapes in the play, one at the end of each act, and they definitely establish Macheath as a Jack Sheppard, the escape artist. In the first two escapes, it is Polly and Lucy, respectively, who enable Macheath to avoid the law, and they do it out of love. In the third case it is the taste of the town that helps Macheath escape the gallows and poetical justice, perhaps also out of love. It is an over-determined ending: poetical justice would have him hanged; the generic and "unnatural" laws of sentimental comedy and opera would have him saved; the taste of the town would have him saved; "realism" would have him executed. Or would it? It is a curious fact about the eighteenth-century legal system that the increasing extension of the death penalty to offences against property coincided with a more frequent use of the pardon and reprieve. More death sentences led to pardons than to hangings. The eighteenth-century legal system was, as Hay says, a combination of majesty, justice, and mercy, and part of the resistance to the rationalization of the legal code was the immense power created by the royal prerogative to pardon; the majesty exercised power as much in pardoning as in executing, and the former was more useful in maintaining the consent and acquiescence of the governed.

There is a struggle in *The Beggar's Opera* between two types of law, the one represented by the reprieve, the other by poetical justice. It corresponds to the struggle over the rationalization of the law, and to the struggle between two meanings of property, on the one hand the common rights and customary perquisites, and on the other the enclosures and the absolute ownership of property. I have already cited Hay's comment that the rise in crime is in part accounted for by this redefinition of customary rights to use woods and commons as offences. In the play these two types of law also

correspond to two types of honour. First, there is the law and honour of Peachum who says "a lawyer is an honest employment, so
is mine" (1.1). His is a law of counting and contracts, of preying
on one's neighbours. Lockit, in a scene which parallels Peachum's
opening scene, says that "of all the animals of prey, man is the only
sociable one" (3.2). Theirs is a law of self-interest, and one can understand, even admit, their self-assessment as men of honour (the
meaning of honour as "to honour, that is, pay, a bill" has its first
usage, according to OED, in 1706; surely that is Peachum's honour). When Peachum says that "we encourage those who betray
their friends" (2.10), he does not see himself as betraying anyone.
He says that Macheath would understand: "the captain knows, that
as tis his employment to rob, so tis ours to take robbers; every man
to his business" (1.10). But as a code implies a transgression, so the
meaning of betrayal is love, as Polly and Lucy discover when they
betray their fathers.

The other law, the other honour, is that of the gang and Macheath. Macheath is surprised that a member of gang should betray
him; we know that Jenny did not betray Macheath and it enforces
our sense of the honour of the gang. It is a law not of counting but
of extravagance, of personal favours. So after Lockit's song comparing men with pikes, preying on their friends, Macheath sings a
lament about the erosive effect of money on friendship (3.4). Macheath gives away money, and tells Matt not to rob the "fellow with
a brown coat with a narrow gold binding"; "he's a good honest
kind of fellow, and one of us" (3.4). The betrayal implied in this
code of honour is mercenary; so Macheath's betrayal of Polly and
Lucy for other women is an extravagance within that code.

The escapes that end each act are ruled by the law of custom,
not contract; it is against any economy for them to be allowed; they
all come from love, rather like the benevolent king's pardon. The
reprieve in particular should be looked at. Fielding has a reprieve in
Jonathan Wild but it is not extravagant: first of all it reprieves a totally innocent man; second, a clear reason is given for it. As the nar-
rator says:

> Lest our reprieve should seen to resemble that in the *Beg-
> gar's Opera,* I shall endeavour to show [the reader] that
> this incident, which is undoubtedly true, is at least as nat-
> ural as delightful; for we assure him we would rather

have suffered half mankind to be hanged than have saved one contrary to the strictest rules of writing and probability.

Beggars and thieves are not bound by contract, but by paternalism, customs, ancient rights, a discretionary system of law. The new system of Peachum would replace these rights with counting, with a rationalized law, indeed with the bourgeois morality that triumphs in Fielding's comic morality play in prose. So far from being a resolution into a protoromantic cult of independence and individualism, it is a defence of English custom (and here we see how the *Opera* might be seen as an affirmation of both the pardon *and* the spectacle of hanging).

The great strength of *The Beggar's Opera* is that this defence is not one of genteel English custom but manages to make an odd union of the aristocracy and the people. And here we are faced with Empson's other comment, that the play breaks through the class system and creates a greater unity. Though I think this is the overall effect of the play (and another part of its continuing popularity), it seems slightly more complicated than Empson puts it. For in my account of the royal pardon, the reader may have noted a slip: the reprieve in the *Opera* is not a royal one at all; it is granted by the "rabble," the "taste of the town." It is a very artificial representation of the riots at hangings that both Foucault and Hay tell us the authorities feared, when the "rabble" would take justice into their hands and reverse the sentence. The spectacle of hanging, the display of the power and authority of the state, could also become the occasion for rebellion against that authority. Certainly Gay did not intend, as Brecht did, that the play should lead the audience to revolution; but as a corollary to Empson's idea of the play creating class unity, I will cite a suggestive comment by Foucault:

> Perhaps we should see this literature of crime, which proliferated around a few exemplary figures [Foucault's footnote cites Wild and Sheppard as well as French examples], neither as a spontaneous form of "popular expression," nor as a concerted programme of propaganda and moralization from above; it was the locus in which two investments of penal practice met—a sort of battleground around the crime, its punishment and its memory.

The Beggar's Opera seems to me one such locus of contrary investments, of party satire, popular speech, fashionable opera, and two codes of law and honour. And this is why it does not have a proper happy ending, why the hero is not really moral, why the unity is incomplete. The comedy seems a straightforward youth vs. age plot; however, it is curiously inverted. For the new system, the growing, thriving commercial capitalism, is figured as the parents, and the children act out the part of an impotent and parasitic aristocracy, now more and more aligning itself with the money-lenders (who Macheath advises robbing—3.4). The aristocracy may be a figure for total villainy, as in Fielding, but it is difficult in the eighteenth century for even Gay, a hanger-on of the aristocracy, to create a real hero from it. Macheath and Polly cannot win—without the artificial intervention of the rabble.

The Beggar as Incompetent Poet

John Fuller

Gay's next play [after *The Captives*] happily returned to the kind of burlesque he had already brilliantly exploited in *The What D'Ye Call It,* substituting a metropolitan for a rustic milieu. The pastoral origins of *The Beggar's Opera* (produced at Lincoln's Inn Fields on January 29, 1728) are not perhaps wholly obvious, but the first hint does go back a dozen years earlier to the time when the pastoral controversy was still alive and Gay was ready to poke fun at writers inept at literary decorum. Swift wrote to Pope on August 30, 1716, that Gay might try his hand at a set of Quaker pastorals (which he did) and went on to remark: "I believe further, the personal ridicule is not exhausted; and that a porter, foot-man, or chair-man's pastoral might do well. Or what think you of a Newgate pastoral, among the whores and thieves there?" When Gay saved this idea up for a comedy and mentioned to Swift that he had begun work on it, the latter was, surprisingly, not much impressed. Gay, however, persisted. He no doubt felt that even if purely formal or stylistic burlesque was somewhat played out, the dramatic possibilities inherent in the mock-genre were not. He seems to have borrowed some of *The What D'Ye Call It*'s most absurdly touching scenes in the initial shaping of his plot. Once again we have a criminal awaiting execution and behaving like a tragic hero. Again there is the prolonged and elevated emotional parting of a pair of socially insignificant lovers. Again there is a reprieve, and the visible stage-managing of the play within the play by its author.

One of the literary allusions in the earlier work, the rivalry of

From *John Gay: Dramatic Works* (vol. 1), edited by John Fuller. © 1983 by John Fuller. The Clarendon Press, 1983.

Kitty and Dorcas evoking that of Statira and Roxana for Alexander the Great in Lee's *The Rival Queens,* is taken up again in the rivalry of Polly and Lucy for Macheath's affections (a situation seized upon by Hogarth in his famous engraving of act 3, scene 11 as the quintessence of the plot). Such an allusion is a happy one for *The Beggar's Opera,* conceived as it partly was as burlesque of the Italian opera: Handel's *Alessandro,* produced on May 5, 1726, had been specially written for Faustina Bordoni's London debut and was designed to show off her and Cuzzoni's talents to contrasted advantage. As Bronson points out, this opera has some general resemblance to *The Beggar's Opera* in Alessandro's vacillation between Rossane and Lisaura, and in their own discussion of their mutual unhappiness. At any rate, Macheath clearly impressed himself upon Swift as a kind of raffish Alexander the Great; too late, on March 28, 1728, he wrote to Gay with a suggestion quite in the required spirit of literary parody: "I wish Mackheath when he was going to be hang'd had imitated Alexdr the great when he was dying. I would have had his fellow rogues, desire his commands about a Successor, and he to answer, let it be the most worthy: & c."

Earlier hints may have been supplied by Pope, since much of the play was written at his house, but in general one receives the impression that Gay maintained the habit of independence acquired during the writing of his tragedies. Pope in fact denied collaboration beyond the altering of an expression here and there. It was Gay, after all, who was addicted to city pleasures and who may have actually had the contacts in the underworld necessary to paint convincing portraits of highwayman, pickpocket, fence, and gaoler. The affairs of the most notorious criminals of the age were, of course, no secret to the public at large, being already the subject of ballads, popular biographies, or stage mimes. Gay himself had written "Newgate's Garland," a ballad about Joseph ("Blueskin") Blake's attempt to cut Jonathan Wild's throat when on trial at the Old Bailey. It was sung in the third scene of Thurmond's mime *Harlequin Sheppard* (1724) which celebrated Jack Sheppard's sensational escape from Newgate prison. Sheppard was treated as a hero by the crowds when he was finally hanged (compare *The Beggar's Opera,* 1.12). It was the activities of gangsters like Blake, Sheppard, and Wild in the early 1720s that must have turned Gay's mind to the underworld as a subject for *The Beggar's Opera:* Sheppard and Wild were direct models for Macheath and Peachum, while Lockit appears to have been conceived as an amalgam of Charles Hitchen (Under City-Marshal) and Spurling, the Newgate turnkey. An anecdote in *The Flying-Post* for January 11, 1729, suggests that Gay, meeting Wild by chance in a Windsor hotel, pretended to be a thief himself and thereby managed to extract a great deal of useful information from "the genuine Peachum." If we are inclined to treat such gossip with circumspection, it is at least true that Gay himself wrote of going to Newgate "to finish my scenes the more correctly." The play was finished by October 22, 1727, and was shown to Congreve and to Voltaire.

Gay's friends were not confident of the play's success, but he pressed on with it. He was smarting under his recent failure to obtain a decent position at Court after attempting to win favour with such works as *The Captives* and the *Fables,* and was in just the right mood to persevere with a work which seemed to everyone to be a doubtful novelty. He could later congratulate himself that he had (in contrast to *The Captives,* perhaps) "push'd through this precarious Affair without servility or flattery." Cibber turned the play down for Drury Lane, perhaps not entirely for personal reasons. The Duke of Queensberry remarked, when shown the play: "This is a very odd thing, Gay; I am satisfied that it is either a very good thing, or a very bad thing," echoing Congreve who had said that "it would either take greatly, or be damned confoundedly." The view was to a degree shared by John Rich, manager of Lincoln's Inn Fields, who ultimately produced it.

In the event it did take greatly. It is Gay's most celebrated play, and more has been written about it than about the rest of his work put together. I cannot pretend to deal with it more than cursorily in this context, and the interested reader is directed to Schultz's detailed account. Undoubtedly its great success was due to its novel use of songs sung to popular airs which Gay chose himself, fitting to them lyrics which meaningfully elaborated upon the themes of the play. Gay had used songs in his plays before, but never so extensively. There was ample precedent for the use of popular tunes of the day in dramatic works. Thomas Duffet's "Epilogue in the manner of Macbeth," added to a burlesque of Settle's *The Empress of Morocco* (1673), does so. *The Rehearsal* (1672) uses broadside ballads, and Gay admired D'Urfey's *Wonders in the Sun* (1706). Perhaps his principal model was, however, the *comédie en vaudeville* of the Théâtre de la Foire in Paris, where from the 1690s ballads to familiar tunes had been used to parody the operas of Lully and others. Originally no accompaniment to the songs was intended, until Rich suggested it on the second last rehearsal and the Duchess of Queensberry insisted upon it. At this stage the composer Pepusch was brought in to arrange the tunes, and to provide an overture. Pepusch was in his early sixties at the time, a respected composer and used to working in the theatre. Gay no doubt admired his *Apollo and Daphne* (1716), to words by Hughes, since his own libretto for *Acis and Galatea* owes much to it.

It is not known whether Handel, already a friend and collaborator of Gay's, had been approached first. It seems, on the face of it, hardly likely that he could have worked with much enjoyment on an enterprise designed in some measure to make fun of the very kind of entertainment he was most concerned with in these years. And yet Gay's parody of Italian opera is not as central to the play as has sometimes been supposed, and may represent comparatively late thoughts in his conception of the piece. The principal parodic elements are openly discussed in the Beggar's framing scenes, and it is to the framing device that the title draws attention. Similarly, some aspects of musical burlesque found in the Overture and in some of the songs would be entirely due to the musical arrangement, known to be a last-minute matter. In many cases where the characters, incidents, or structure of the play itself seem to owe something to *Alessandro* or to other Italian operas, there is a sufficient source in the ordinary tragic stage of the period, which of course Gay was well-used to mocking (but see Bronson). If he felt that his own tragedies had been less than successful, he would have had an idea of what to blame. The new music was a threat to tragedy, finding an easy (and predominantly female) ear, as the epilogue to *The Captives* ruefully observes:

> All Ladies love the play that moves the most.
> Ev'n in this house I've known some tender fair,
> Touch'd with meer sense alone, confess a tear.
> But the soft voice of an *Italian* wether,
> Makes them all languish three whole hours together.
> And where's the wonder? Plays, like Mass, are
>   sung,
> (Religious *Drama*)!—in an unknown tongue.
>
>   (ll. 16–22)

This sentiment is echoed by Lady Ninny in *The Rehearsal at Goatham,* 5.89. A little earlier Gay had extended the cultural damage to the whole of classical literature: "People have now forgot Homer, and Virgil & Caesar, or at least they have lost their ranks, for in London and Westminster in all polite conversation's Senesino is daily voted to be the greatest man that ever liv'd." Senesino was, of course, a castrato. Macheath's bountiful sexuality restores the heroic status quo: at least in this sense Macheath is a "great man." We must judge the extent of operatic parody by what we can find in the text: in this connection it is interesting to note that Bronson, who is the most detailed commentator in this respect, does not think that the play is a serious attack on Italian opera and the absence of satire upon extravagant devices of staging or upon incomprehensible libretti would support the view. Certainly the burlesque is neither extensive nor ill-natured, and Handel bore no grudge, even though the tearaway success of *The Beggar's Opera* meant a loss of audience for the "outlandish" opera. The *Somerset House Gazette* records a rather dry exchange between Pepusch and Handel:

> P: I hope, sir, you do not include me amongst those who did injustice to your talents.
>
> H: Nod at all, nod at all, God forbid! I am a great admirer of the airs of "The Beggar's Opera" andt every professional gendtleman must do his best for to live.

Gay had indeed done his best this time, and was able to repair the ravages of the South Sea Bubble, earning £693 13*s.* 6*d.* from the production alone. The familiar joke that the play had made Rich gay and Gay rich was coined by *The Craftsman* no. 83 as early as February 3. By February 12 all the boxes had been booked to the twenty-fifth night, and even the author himself was proud of his ability to obtain tickets. The play ran for an unprecedented sixty-two nights, Gay's portrait was engraved, the actress playing the part of Polly became the toast of the town despite being inaudible and ran away with the Duke of Bolton. The circumstances of the play's reception and popularity are well-known. It inaugurated a vogue for the ballad-opera which lasted for eight years, and was a direct influence upon the German *Singspiele* of the 1750s. The proceeds enabled Rich to set about building Covent Garden.

The immediate success of the play owed much to its musical

charm and to the character of Polly (as Boswell's story of the first audience's response to air 12 suggests) but its role as a *cause célèbre* was undoubtedly due to its social and political satire. "Does W——think you intended an affront to him in your opera," wrote Swift on February 26, 1728. "Pray God he may." Despite the fact that the play is by no means a *pièce à clef,* he may be thought to have had good enough reason. Gay first establishes taxation as a form of highway robbery in the allusion to Walpole at 1.3.28 as "Robin of Bagshot, alias Gorgon, alias Bluff Bob, alias Carbuncle, alias Bob Booty," reinforcing the point by making Macheath the highwayman his hero ("by this Character every Body will understand *One,* who makes it his Business arbitrarily to *levy* and *collect* Money on the People for his *own Use,* and of which he always dreads to give *any Account*"). Macheath's embarrassment at the rival claims of Polly and Lucy was taken to glance at Walpole's relationship with Lady Walpole and with his mistress, Molly Skerret, and the *Key* later points out the sobriquet of "Great Man" as another significant link. Yet Gay pulls this particular punch by first of all presenting Peachum, the thief-catcher and fence, at the centre of a web of self-aggrandizement and multiple deception that had an immediate and much stronger political impact, underlined by his first song ("*And the Statesman, because he's so great, / Thinks his Trade as honest as mine*"). Peachum was based upon Jonathan Wild, and the equation Wild = Walpole had already been established by *Mist's Weekly Journal,* June 12 and 19, 1725. The *Key* says that Peachum and Lockit can be linked as Walpole and his brother-in-law Townshend, a relationship apparently supported by the quarrel at 2.10. At this point, however, the parallels become unclear. It is Lockit (played by Jack Hall, "a very *corpulent, bulky* Man") who according to this theory is labelled the "*prime Minister of Newgate.*" Peachum was played by John Hippisley as "a *little, awkward slovenly* Fellow." Moreover, as Schultz points out, the famous quarrel at Cleveland Court between Walpole and Townshend is misdated by Cooke when he gives an account of it in his *Memoirs of Macklin,* and could not therefore have been a model for the Peachum/Lockit quarrel, even though earlier quarrels may have been. The author of the *Key* prefers to think that Macheath, "who hath also a *goodly Presence,* and hath a tolerable *Bronze* upon his Face," represents Walpole. In this way the political parallels subtly shift, offering a slightly different perspective from each viewpoint. A recent article even claims Macheath as George II and Lucy as the Countess of Suffolk. If Mrs Howard were indeed in Gay's mind at the time, it would be much more likely to be as the agent of his disappointed hopes of Court preferment. Such disappointment (he had refused the by no means totally ignominious appointment of Gentleman-Usher to the Princess Louisa the previous October, an appropriate office for a poet who had just written his *Fables* for another royal child) might well have been what directed his attention to Walpole, however, who believed that Gay had once libelled him, had reported as much to the Queen, and was no doubt responsible for the supposed meagreness of the office. Gay's friends were already aligned behind Bolingbroke and the Dawley group against Walpole: the success of *The Beggar's Opera* left no doubt that Gay was of their company. Walpole himself encored and applauded air 30 when the first-night audience obviously felt that it was directed against him, and took no action against the play. This was a statesmanlike quick-wittedness worthy of Bolingbroke's turning of *Cato* to the Tory account fifteen years before. Gay himself lost his Whitehall lodgings, originally granted to him by the Earl of Lincoln, and even found his letters being read by the post office, but was otherwise not unduly persecuted: his position as Lottery Commissioner, for instance, continued from 1722 to 1731. However, stage attacks on Walpole's administration intensified in the years after *The Beggar's Opera*, and Gay's sequel, *Polly,* was not allowed to be performed.

There is a sense in which the burlesque tragedy of *The What D'Ye Call It* is wholly appropriate. When the steward of a country house comes to put on a play which he has presumably written himself he will want it to sound as sublime as Lee or Banks, even though the only serious events that he knows anything at all about are of purely local significance: poaching, conscription, and unwanted pregnancies. Similarly, when a beggar comes to write an opera (to celebrate the marriage of two ballad-singers) he knows nothing of Alexander the Great, but everything about the criminals who rule the underworld he inhabits. The wedded pair would have wanted to hear ballads, naturally, and this accounts for the novelty of Gay's extensive use of ballad tunes, but they would also have wanted an opera about the leaders of organized crime to whom they very likely themselves owed allegiance:

> Let not the ballad-singer's shrilling strain
> Amid the swarm thy list'ning ear detain:
> Guard well thy pocket; for these *Syrens* stand
> To aid the labours of the diving hand;
> Confed'rate in the cheat, they draw the throng,
> And cambrick handkerchiefs reward the song.
>
> (*Trivia* 3.77–82)

It is thus that Brecht made use of mendicant beggars in *Die Dreigro-schenoper,* lending a further social realism to the Edwardian Soho which was his particular version of Gay's underworld. Benjamin Britten's adaptation also introduced beggars, but softened their criminal function.

However, Gay's Beggar is not only a representative of this underworld, as his very first words show: "If Poverty be a Title to Poetry, I am sure No-body can dispute mine." The claim is proverbial, but Gay intends to suggest that since most poets are incompetent they will make no money out of their work. The Beggar is "really" therefore (as indeed he is openly in the introduction to *Polly*) simply a poet, and a bad one, since he is incompetent in handling genres. The same point was more elaborately made by Pope in *The Dunciad:* the Cave of Poverty and Poetry is a place where, among other lapses of decorum, "Tragedy and Comedy embrace" (bk. 1, l. 69) and where, therefore, the Beggar's notion of presenting an opera about criminals would appear quite acceptable. In the correct world it is not, and that is why he is a beggar.

Gay's "modern" preface to *The What D'Ye Call It* proposed that "*the Sentiments of Princes and Clowns have not in reality that difference which they seem to have.*" A recipe for literary disaster if taken seriously, this notion is the very backbone of the social satire in *The Beggar's Opera.* "Through the whole Piece," claims the Beggar in the penultimate scene, "you may observe such a similitude of Manners in high and low Life, that it is difficult to determine whether (in the fashionable Vices) the fine Gentlemen imitate the Gentlemen of the Road, or the Gentlemen of the Road the fine Gentlemen." Gay had been musing on this identity for some time. In 1717 he (or possibly Pope) presented Cadogan as a parvenu and a cut-purse in *Horace, Epod. IV, Imitated By Sir James Baker, Kt. To Lord Cad—n,* and in August 1723 he wrote to Mrs. Howard: "I cannot indeed wonder that the Talents requisite for a great Statesman are so scarce in the world since so many of those who possess them are every month cut off in the prime of their Age at the Old-Baily." Kerby-Miller notes [in his edition of *Martinus Scriblerus*] a probable hint for *The Beggar's Opera* in chapter 12 of *The Memoirs of Martinus Scriblerus:* "He did not doubt likewise to find the same resemblance in Highway-men and Conquerors," and Gay may also have remembered his early farce *The Mohocks,* where the town rowdies comport themselves like epic heroes and the whores have unusually polite manners. When, in *The Beggar's Opera,* the highwaymen, prostitutes, and fences speak and act like politicians, court ladies, and lawyers, their ambiguous social position yields infinite variations on the kind of moral inversion which Gay wishes to explore.

The qualities which an opera might be expected to take seriously (love, ambition, loyalty) are continually undermined by the paradoxical assumptions of characters who wear their criminality with an air of gracefulness, fashion, or practicality. Peachum, who has a vast organization for the reception of stolen property, and yet who also makes money by informing on the thieves whose talents he employs, justifies his moral position by comparing it with that of a lawyer: "Like me too he acts in a double Capacity, both against Rogues and for 'em; for 'tis but fitting that we should protect and encourage Cheats, since we live by them" (1.1.10). All our moral expectations are therefore reversed in Peachum's world. And yet the closeness to the puritanical and hypocritical bourgeois ethic remains, and is credible enough to give his paradoxes the full sting of moral satire. His long speech at 1.4.75, for instance, exposes a father's economic interest in his daughter as ingeniously as possible without being downright macabre. Peachum is running a family business, but we are reminded that any family is a business of a kind, and the rationale of social pimping provides a solid basis for a number of good jokes about marriage in the following scenes (for example, at 1.8.12: "Married! . . . Do you think your Mother and I should have liv'd comfortably so long together, if ever we had been married?"). Polly, who has married for love, will not care that a highwayman might treat her just as badly as a Lord. She is well versed in the romances that Macheath has been lending her, and these tell her that "none of the great Heroes were ever false in Love" (1.13.16). With Polly played straight, the burlesque of pathetic tragedy and victimization becomes a rather more equilibrist exercise than in the case of Kitty and Filbert, so that while we can see very well that she is being used to burlesque sentimentalism, she remains at the same time a true creature of sentiment, and her love for Macheath is indeed genuine. With her predicament at once amusing and moving us, one of the most absurdly touching scenes in the play is when her rival Lucy Lockit decides that she is simply not happy enough to deserve to be poisoned. The very precariousness of happiness is one of the important thematic under-currents of the play ("A Moment of time may make us unhappy for-ever," 2.15.30) so to grasp it boldly in the face of calculated opposition becomes really heroic. Polly's love is one of the very few reliable ideals in a world of particularly unreliable concrete things (like missing property or double-dealing employers) so that our feelings are taxed when her lofty emotion is bestowed upon a robber and multiple bigamist whom most other characters in the play wish at one time or another to betray.

Gay makes sure, then, that we are attracted to Macheath as well, and does so by lending him an aristocratic swagger that contrasts favourably with the dogged book-keeping of Peachum (for an extended discussion of the subtle social implications of this contrast, see chapter 6 of William Empson's *Some Versions of Pastoral*, 1935 [reprinted in this volume], the best criticism that the play has had). Our assent to the Player's objections to Macheath's being hanged in the penultimate scene is an assent assiduously worked toward. It goes beyond a burlesque of the happy endings of operas, although the happy ending was a particularly vulnerable development in serious drama in the eighteenth century, and it was one which Brecht was still eager to satirize when producing his version of the opera almost exactly two hundred years later. It is appropriate, perhaps, where the victim is not the villain, but has been manipulated by the real villains of the piece. One of the reasons, no doubt, for the undercurrent of moral protest about the play throughout the eighteenth century, from Justice Fielding and others like him, was the attractiveness of Macheath, though as Dr Johnson remarks in his *Life of Gay*: "It is not possible for anyone to imagine that he may rob with safety because he sees Macheath reprieved upon the stage." The amoral hero was not new, of course. A contemporary portrait of the actor Thomas Walker as Macheath describes the character as "a second Dorimant" and emphasizes those manly qualities which appeal to the ladies. *Memoirs . . . of Captain Mackheath* underlines in more detail this debt to Etherege, and is perhaps worth quoting at some length:

The Dramatick Writer has indeed dress'd him out to Advantage, he stands erect the first Piece in the Canvas, and has gained much popular Applause; he has made him the Lover and the Warrior, he is the Darling of the Fair, and the Glory of the thievish Heroes who surround him: He is a perfect, polite, modern fine Gentleman, and *Dorimant* in Sir *Fopling,* though a Person of equal Morals, is not a more accomplish'd Rake. He commits his Robberies with an Air of Authority and Gallantry, the common People mistake his Vice for Virtues; and those who are not in his Gang, applaud him.

It was thus clearly a mistake in a production in 1777 to introduce a scene in which Macheath is sent to the hulks for three years, even though, as we understand from Gay's own sequel, transportation is the result of the Player's and the Beggar's intervention. Macheath's charm must seem sufficient to show him rising buoyantly above any of the conventional demands of justice. Once really transported, the authority and gallantry of the rake are utterly destroyed. This is clear enough from *Polly,* where Macheath is discovered living ignominiously in disguise in the West Indies with only one prostitute. He even betrays his gang. This is not behaviour worthy of a hero, and in his sequel Gay was able, without any risk of rebuke from "the taste of the town," to kill him off and marry Polly to the Noble Savage, Cawwawkee.

Chronology

1685	John Gay born June 30 in Barnstable, Devon.
c. 1695	Attends Barnstable Grammar School.
1702	Becomes apprentice to a silk mercer in London.
1707	Becomes secretary to Aaron Hill.
1708	First poem, *Wine,* published.
1711	Beginning of friendship with Pope. *The Present State of Wit* is published.
1712	*The Mohocks* published. Gay becomes domestic steward for the Duchess of Monmouth.
1713	"Scriblerus Club" formed with Gay as secretary. *Rural Sports, The Fan* published. *The Wife of Bath* produced.
1714	*The Shepherd's Week* published. Gay is secretary to Lord Clarendon on his diplomatic mission to Hanover. *A Letter to a Lady* published.
1715	*The What D'Ye Call It* produced and published.
1716	*Trivia; or, The Art of Walking the Streets of London* published.
1717	*Three Hours after Marriage* produced and published. Gay travels to Paris and Aix.
1719	*Acis and Galatea,* set to music by Handel, performed at the estate of the Duke of Chandos.
1720	Publication of *Poems on Several Occasions* brings Gay a large profit, which he invests and loses in the South Sea Bubble.
1721	*A Panegyrical Epistle to Mr. Thomas Snow* published.
1723	Becomes Commissioner of State Lottery.
1724	*The Captives* produced and published.
1725	*To a Lady on her Passion for Old China, Newgate's Garland* published.

1726   Visited by Swift for much of summer.

1727   *Fables,* first series, published. Gay offered and refuses post as Gentleman Usher to Princess Louisa.

1728   *The Beggar's Opera* opens January 29 at Lincoln's Inn Fields and is a great success. Gay writes *Polly,* a sequel, which is refused license for performance.

1729   *Polly* published. Gay loses apartments at Whitehall and lives with Duke and Duchess of Queensberry.

1730   *The Wife of Bath* published and produced.

1732   *Acis and Galatea* produced and the libretto alone published. Gay dies December 3 and is buried in Westminster Abbey.

1733   *Achilles* published and produced.

1734   *The Distress'd Wife* produced.

1737   The Stage Licensing Act enacted.

1738   *Fables,* second series, published.

1743   *The Distress'd Wife* published.

1754   *The Rehearsal at Goatham* published.

1777   *Polly* first produced.

Contributors

HAROLD BLOOM, Sterling Professor of the Humanities at Yale University, is the author of *The Anxiety of Influence, Poetry and Repression,* and many other volumes of literary criticism. His forthcoming study, *Freud: Transference and Authority,* attempts a full-scale reading of all of Freud's major writings. A MacArthur Prize Fellow, he is general editor of five series of literary criticism published by Chelsea House. During 1987–88, he served as Charles Eliot Norton Professor of Poetry at Harvard University.

WILLIAM EMPSON was one of the most eminent of modern poet-critics. He taught for many years in China, and later at Sheffield University. His principal writings include his *Collected Poems, Seven Types of Ambiguity, Some Versions of Pastoral* and *The Structure of Complex Words.*

MARTIN PRICE is Sterling Professor of English at Yale University. His books include *Swift's Rhetorical Art: A Study in Structure and Meaning, To the Palace of Wisdom: Studies in Order and Energy from Dryden to Blake,* and a number of edited volumes on literature of the seventeenth, eighteenth, and nineteenth centuries. His most recent book is *Forms of Life: Character and Moral Imagination in the Novel.*

PATRICIA MEYER SPACKS is Professor of English at Yale University. Her books include *The Adolescent Idea: Myths of Youth and the Adult Imagination, The Female Imagination, Imagining a Self, John Gay,* and *Gossip.*

RONALD PAULSON is Professor of English at The Johns Hopkins University. His books include *Popular and Polite Art in the Age of Hogarth and Fielding, Literary Landscape: Turner and Constable, Book and Play: Shakespeare, Milton, and the Bible,* and *Representations of Revolution.*

WILLIAM A. MCINTOSH is Professor of English at the U.S. Military Academy, West Point.

PETER LEWIS is Lecturer in English at the University of Durham. He is the author of *John Gay:* The Beggar's Opera, and editor of *Radio Drama* and a critical edition of *The Beggar's Opera.*

MICHAEL DENNING is Professor of American Studies at Yale University.

JOHN FULLER, Lecturer and Tutor in English at Magdalen College, Oxford, is the author of *W. H. Auden* as well as volumes of his own poetry. He has edited the plays of John Gay.

Bibliography

Armens, Sven M. *John Gay: Social Critic*. New York: Kings Crown Press, 1954.

Bateson, F. W. *English Comic Drama, 1700–1750*. 1929. Reprint. New York: Russell & Russell, 1963.

Berger, Arthur V. "*The Beggar's Opera,* the Burlesque, and Italian Opera." *Music and Letters* 17 (1936): 93–105.

Bloom, Edward A., and Lillian D. Bloom. *Satire's Persuasive Voice*. Ithaca: Cornell University Press, 1979.

Boas, Frederick S. *An Introduction to 18th-Century Drama*. Oxford: Oxford University Press, 1953.

Bronson, Bertrand Harris. "*The Beggar's Opera.*" In *Facets of the Enlightenment: Studies in English Literature and Its Contexts,* 60–90. Berkeley and Los Angeles: University of California Press, 1968.

Burgess, C. F. "Political Satire: John Gay's *The Beggar's Opera.*" *Midwest Quarterly* 6 (1965): 265–276.

———, ed. *The Letters of John Gay*. Oxford: Oxford University Press, 1966.

Clinton-Baddely, V. C. *The Burlesque Tradition in the English Theatre after 1660*. London: Methuen, 1952.

Donaldson, Ian. " 'A Double Capacity': *The Beggar's Opera.*" In *The World Upside-down,* 159–82. Oxford: Oxford University Press, 1970.

Downie, J. A. "The Poet's Foe." In *Britain in the Age of Walpole,* edited by Jeremy Black, 171–88. New York: Macmillan, 1984.

Erskine-Hill, Howard. "The Significance of Gay's Drama." In *English Drama: Form and Development,* edited by Marie Axton and Raymond Williams, 142–63. Cambridge: Cambridge University Press, 1977.

Forsgren, Adina. *John Gay: "Poet of a Lower Order."* Stockholm: Natur och Kultur, 1964.

Gagey, Edmond McAdoo. *Ballad Opera*. New York: Columbia University Press, 1937.

Goldgar, Bertrand A. *Walpole and the Wits*. Lincoln: University of Nebraska Press, 1976.

Griffith, Benjamin W., Jr. Introduction to *The Beggar's Opera,* edited by Benjamin W. Griffith, Jr., 5–50. New York: Barrons Educational Series, 1962.

Hughes, Leo. *The Drama's Patrons: A Study of the Eighteenth-Century London Audience*. Austin: University of Texas Press, 1971.

Irving, William Henry. *John Gay: Favorite of the Wits*. Durham, N.C.: Duke University Press, 1940.

Kephart, Carolyn. "An Unnoticed Forerunner of *The Beggar's Opera*." *Music and Letters* 61 (1980): 266–71.

Kern, Jean B. *Dramatic Satire in the Age of Walpole: 1720–1750*. Ames: Iowa State University Press, 1976.

———. "A Note on *The Beggar's Opera*." *Philological Quarterly* 17 (1938): 411–13.

Kidson, Frank. The Beggar's Opera: *Its Predecessors and Successors*. London: Cambridge University Press, 1922.

Kramnick, Isaac. *Bolingbroke and His Circle*. Cambridge: Harvard University Press, 1968.

Lewis, Peter. "The Abuse of Language in *The Beggar's Opera*." *The British Journal for Eighteenth-Century Studies* 4, no. 1 (1981): 44–53.

———. *John Gay: The Beggar's Opera*. London: E. Arnold, 1976.

———. "The Uncertainty Principle in *The Beggar's Opera*." *Durham University Journal* 72 (1980): 143–46.

———, ed. *The Beggar's Opera*. Edinburgh: Oliver & Boyd, 1973.

Lindgren, Lowell. "*Camilla* and *The Beggar's Opera*." *Philological Quarterly* 59, no. 1 (1980): 44–61.

Loftis, John. *The Politics of Drama in Augustan England*. Oxford: Oxford University Press, 1963.

Mack, Maynard. "Gay: *The Beggar's Opera*." In the Introduction to *The Augustans*, edited by Maynard Mack, 17–19. Englewood Cliffs, N.J.: Prentice-Hall, 1961.

Noble, Yvonne, ed. *Twentieth-Century Interpretations of* The Beggar's Opera: *A Collection of Critical Essays*. Englewood Cliffs, N.J.: Prentice-Hall, 1975.

Novak, Maximillian E. "Scriblerian Satire." In *Eighteenth-Century English Literature*. New York: Schocken, 1983.

Paulson, Ronald. *Popular and Polite Art in the Age of Hogarth and Fielding*. London: University of Notre Dame Press, 1979.

———. *Hogarth: His Life and Times,* vol. 1. New Haven: Yale University Press, 1971.

Preston, John. "The Ironic Mode: A Comparison of *Jonathan Wild* and *The Beggar's Opera*." *Essays in Criticism* 16 (1966): 268–80.

Roberts, Edgar V., ed. *The Beggar's Opera*. Lincoln: University of Nebraska Press, 1969.

Schultz, William Eben. Gay's Beggar's Opera, *Its Content, History and Influence*. New Haven: Yale University Press, 1923.

Sherwin, J. J. "The World is Mean and Man Uncouth." *Virginia Quarterly Review* 35 (1959): 258–70.

Sherwin, Oscar. *Mr. Gay*. New York: John Day, 1929.

Sillars, S. J. "Musical Iconography in *The Beggar's Opera*." *The British Journal for Eighteenth-Century Studies* 1, no. 3 (1978): 182–85.

Spacks, Patricia Meyer. "John Gay: A Satirist's Progress." *Essays in Criticism* 14 (1964): 156–70.

Stevens, David Harrison. "Some Immediate Effects of *The Beggar's Opera*." In *The Manly Anniversary Studies in Language and Literature,* 180–89. Chicago: University of Chicago Press, 1923.

Sutherland, James. "John Gay." In *Pope and His Contemporaries: Essays Presented to George Sherburn,* edited by James L. Clifford and Louis A. Landa, 201–14. Oxford: Clarendon Press, 1949.

Weisstein, Ulrich. "Brecht's Victorian Version of Gay: Imitation and Originality in *Dreigroschenoper.*" *Comparative Literature Studies* 7 (1970): 314–35.

Wertheim, Albert. "Captain Macheath and Polly Peachum in the New World: John Gay and Peter Spacks." *Maske und Kothurn* 27, nos. 2/3 (1981): 176–84.

Acknowledgments

"*The Beggar's Opera:* Mock-pastoral as the Cult of Independence" by William Empson from *Some Versions of Pastoral* by William Empson, © 1960 by New Directions. Reprinted by permission.

"Mercenary Fathers, Possessive Daughters, and Macheath" (originally entitled "Orders and Forms") by Martin Price from *To the Palace of Wisdom: Studies in Order and Energy from Dryden to Blake* by Martin Price, © 1964 by Martin Price. Reprinted by permission.

"The Beggar's Triumph" by Patricia Meyer Spacks from *John Gay* by Patricia Meyer Spacks, © 1965 by Twayne Publishers, Inc., a division of G. K. Hall & Co., Boston. Reprinted by permission.

"Mock-heroic Irony and the Comedy of Manners" (originally entitled "The Villain of Fielding's Satire") by Ronald Paulson from *Satire and the Novel in Eighteenth Century England* by Ronald Paulson, © 1967 by Yale University. Reprinted by permission of Yale University Press.

"Handel, Walpole, and Gay: The Aims of *The Beggar's Opera*" by William A. McIntosh from *Eighteenth-Century Studies* 7, no. 4 (Summer 1974), with full documentation and explanatory notes, © 1974 by the Regents of the University of California. Reprinted by permission of the author and *Eighteenth-Century Studies*.

"*The Beggar's Opera* as Opera and Anti-opera" by Peter Lewis from *John Gay: The Beggar's Opera* by Peter Lewis, © 1976 by Peter Lewis. Reprinted by permission of the author.

"Beggars and Thieves" by Michael Denning from *Literature and History* 8, no. 1 (Spring 1982), © 1982 by the Thames Polytechnic, London. Reprinted by permission of *Literature and History*.

"The Beggar as Incompetent Poet" (originally entitled "Introduction") by John Fuller from *John Gay: Dramatic Works* (vol. 1), edited by John Fuller, © 1983 by John Fuller. Reprinted by permission.

Index